LAURA TAPPER

What Happens In The End?

One car. Two strangers. A thousand miles to figure it out.

First edition

ISBN: 979-8-9954970-3-5

This book was professionally typeset on Reedsy.
Find out more at reedsy.com

For Greg. You're my favorite.

Contents

Foreword

Content Warning

This novel contains depictions of stalking, assault, and attempted sexual assault. Read with care.

Acknowledgments

Thank you to the friends, family, and random internet strangers who cheered me on while I wrote this story. To everyone who read drafts, offered encouragement, or helped me brainstorm road trip stops: you're the reason this book made it to the finish line.

And a special thank you to my ARC readers. Your early feedback and support meant the world.

One

Airport Disaster

Harper should have known her day was doomed from the start.

First, she slept through her alarm in the too-soft bed of the hotel she booked for one final night in New York. Then, her Uber driver didn't bother waiting, possibly making her late for her 9 am flight. She should have laid out her clothes the night before, but instead, she was left scrambling, yanking on the first thing she could find—black leggings and a wrinkled white t-shirt from the floor.

With barely enough time to swipe on some makeup, she managed to stab herself in the eye with her mascara wand—because of course she did. By the time her second Uber driver finally showed up, she had less than an hour to get to JFK. Which was an impossible feat during New York rush hour. Each red light, every creeping mile, sent her anxiety spiking higher.

But the day wasn't going to get any easier.

It was the end of June; the air was thick with heat and the bustle of busy travelers trying to get a head start on the summer. Harper sprinted from the Uber to the airport entrance with a suitcase in one hand and a bag slung over her shoulder, clutching her one saving grace—a leftover mocha latte from the night before. But some inconsiderate jerk plowed into her without so much as a glance back. The cup slipped from her grip, and in an instant, her shirt went from wrinkled to ruined with sticky coffee soaking through the fabric.

Perfect. Just perfect.

But the moment she stepped into the terminal, a coffee stain became the least of her problems.

Something was wrong.

The usual airport rush—the steady hum of boarding calls, rolling suitcases, and half-awake travelers—had been replaced with something more chaotic. Clusters of people crowded the airline counters, their voices rising in frustration. Employees looked overwhelmed; some were glued to their phones, while others were locked in tense conversations with furious passengers.

Harper's gaze snapped to the overhead monitors, expecting flight updates but all she saw were blank, black screens.

Sweat prickled under her collarbone. That wasn't normal.

As she weaved through the terminal, she spotted the self-check-in kiosks and the growing line of people jabbing uselessly at the frozen touchscreens. A woman beside her let out a string of expletives, while a man waved down an airline worker, his voice sharp with impatience.

Harper's grip tightened on her bag. No working screens. No kiosks. And judging by the snaking lines at security, it seemed no one would be getting through anytime soon.

A bad feeling coiled in her chest.

She flagged down a frazzled airline employee rushing past. "Excuse me—what's going on?"

The woman barely spared her a glance. "The airline networks are down. We're working on it. Please be patient." And with that, she vanished into the crowd.

Harper stood frozen. This couldn't be happening. She had already checked out of New York, both mentally and emotionally. Her sights were set on California, and if she didn't leave today, she wasn't sure she ever would.

Flying was out of the question. That much was clear.

Yanking out her phone, she searched for rental cars. Sold out. Sold out. Sold out.

Her pulse pounded as she scrolled through the listings, hope dwindling with each swipe until one final option appeared on the screen. A beat-up, questionable-looking sedan. Definitely not her first choice… but it was that or nothing. Without hesitation, she hit *Reserve.* A confirmation email pinged in her inbox a second later.

Gripping the handle of her suitcase–silently thanking herself for shipping the rest of her belongings ahead to her friend's apartment—she bolted toward the rental counter.

Another mob. Another crowd. More desperate travelers demanding cars that didn't exist. Harper wasn't about to wait. She pushed forward, elbows jabbing, her murmured apologies swallowed by the sea of impatient voices.

She reached the reserved section but only to find a frustrated-looking guy, deep in conversation with a car rental employee.

He had to be a little over six feet. Harper had dealt with enough guys who exaggerated their height to know that this one was actually pretty tall.

His short, tousled brown hair was a mess of uneven waves, like he'd run a hand through it a dozen times already today. A faint scar cut through the stubble along his right cheek. His t-shirt stretched over well-defined biceps, and under different circumstances, Harper might have taken a moment to admire how well it fit him. But admiring some stranger's physique wasn't on her agenda at the moment. And judging by the tension in his stance, he had bigger concerns, too.

He was speaking rapidly to the employee, frustration sharp in his tone. She responded with a terse nod before vanishing to the back. That's when Harper saw the phone in his hand, and more importantly, what was on his screen.

No. No way. This had to be a mistake. There was no possible way the universe was screwing her over this badly.

The same old, beat-up sedan from her own reservation was glaring up at her in the confirmation email he had pulled up.

"Hey!" she blurted, hurrying to the counter.

The man turned, serious brown eyes locking onto hers.

"Excuse me?"

"That's my car." She shoved her phone forward with the reservation email displayed in bold print.

A flicker of tension crossed his features as he looked from her screen to his. With a sharp exhale, he flipped his phone around to show her.

"No. It's mine." He jabbed a finger at the timestamp. "I booked it."

Harper shook her head. "I reserved it *minutes* ago."

His jaw flexed. "Doesn't matter. I'm taking the car." He turned away, dismissing her outright.

Not a chance.

Her pulse pounded. "I need this car. You don't understand–I

have to leave New York today. My new job starts soon."

For a split second, something flickered in his expression, something almost hesitant. Then it was gone.

The man exhaled sharply, clearly exasperated. "You can be as mad as you want, but the keys are mine."

Their eyes locked, tension thick between them, the employee returning with the keys at that moment. She hesitated, glancing between them.

"Uh… is there a problem?"

Harper jumped in. "Yes. *He's* trying to take my car." She waved her phone at the employee. "I have a confirmed reservation. Look."

She frowned, glancing between them. "Sir, can I see your reservation again?"

The man's patience was running thin, but he still held out his phone.

Her face fell. "Oh… no."

Harper felt a sinking feeling. "What?"

The employee sighed wearily. "The car was double-booked."

Harper and the man spoke at the same time. *"Double-booked?"*

The employee gave an apologetic shrug. "I'd offer you another vehicle, but that was our last one. With the airline networks down, we've completely run out."

Harper's pulse pounded. "Please. I have to get to California, and this car is my only option."

The man's expression flickered between surprise and frustration as he glanced down at Harper. "Yeah? And you think *I* don't have somewhere important to be? I can't sit around waiting, either."

Harper narrowed her eyes. "What, late for the annual 'World's Biggest Jerk' convention?"

He scoffed, looking ready to fire back, but the employee cleared her throat. "If you're both going in the same direction… why not share the car?"

Harper recoiled. "Absolutely not. I am *not* spending days trapped in a car with a stranger. Especially *him.*"

The man let out a dry laugh. "Trust me, you're not my first choice either."

The employee, clearly over it, crossed her arms. "Then I'll have to release it to someone else. Decide now."

Harper glanced over her shoulder to see that the crowd of frustrated travelers behind them was swelling by the second. If she let this car go, she'd be right where she started—stranded and at the mercy of flight delays.

She clenched her jaw and huffed, "Fine. I can be the bigger person. We'll share."

The man exhaled sharply, looking as if he hated the idea as much as she did. "Guess I don't have a choice. I'm going to California, too."

Harper blinked. "Where in California?"

His expression darkened, showing clear resentment about having this conversation. "Near Laguna Beach. You?"

"Close that area, too."

He gave a short nod. "We'll figure out the drop-off later."

Harper didn't love the vagueness of that plan, but what choice did she have?

They signed the paperwork in stiff silence. Harper caught his name scrawled in sharp, deliberate letters, *Connor*, his signature practically swallowing hers on the page.

When the employee handed over the keys, Connor snatched them before Harper could react.

"Hey!" she snapped.

He barely glanced at her, but there was the slightest pause before he muttered, 'I'm driving.'

And with that, he grabbed his backpack and suitcase and strode off without another word. Not even bothering to make sure Harper was following him.

She muttered a string of curses under her breath and hurried after him. No way was she letting him take off without her.

When they reached the car, Harper felt a flicker of dismay. It looked even worse in person with faded gray paint. It had to be at least a decade old, maybe two.

Connor popped the trunk, tossed his luggage in, and began shutting it when Harper spoke up.

"Uh, excuse me? I'm putting my suitcase in there, too."

He shot her an unimpressed look. "A 'please' wouldn't kill you."

Only self-control kept her from flipping him off. He lifted the trunk, and she shoved her suitcase inside with a little more force than necessary.

Her frustration had eclipsed her earlier stress, boiling over into pure, seething annoyance.

Harper kept her backpack with her as she climbed into the passenger seat. Connor didn't even wait for her to buckle in before easing the car into the chaotic line of vehicles inching out of the garage.

"Whoa," Harper said, her hand bracing against the dashboard as Connor abruptly hit the brakes.

A horn blared as a black SUV cut in front of them, narrowly missing the hood.

Connor muttered a curse under his breath, his expression hardening. "People drive like psychopaths in this city."

Harper shot him a sideways glance. "Maybe they're trying to

avoid getting sideswiped."

He exhaled slowly through his nose, eyes locked ahead. "I had it under control."

She stayed silent, shifted in her seat, and buckled herself in, stealing a glance at her unwilling companion. His hands clenched the wheel, knuckles white, jaw tight as though suppressing a curse. Harper's eyes drifted to the faint scar on his cheek, then to another along his bicep, both visible on sun-kissed skin.

It hit her: she was about to spend days in a car with a complete stranger. A stranger who looked like he'd been through his share of things. She swallowed hard and broke the heavy silence.

"So," she started, "your name's Connor?"

His head snapped toward her, eyes sharp. "How do you know that?"

Harper blinked. "It was on the paperwork."

"Oh." He faced forward. "Right."

Silence.

Harper scowled. "I'm Harper."

Connor nodded. "Okay."

She stared at him. "Okay? What does that even mean?"

"It means your name is Harper. Got it. Noted." He shot her a sidelong look. "What do you want, a round of applause?"

Her mouth fell open. "Seriously? We'll be stuck in a car together for days, and you don't think knowing each other's names is remotely important?"

Connor exhaled slowly, his fingers brushing over his jaw. "Look, I didn't wake up today planning a cross-country road trip with a stranger. And honestly?" A humorless chuckle escaped him. "I'm really pissed about it. This isn't going to be some movie-style bonding experience."

Harper crossed her arms, sinking into her seat with a glare. "You think I wanted this? The last thing I want is a days-long detour."

Connor didn't respond, eyes locked on the road, but Harper wasn't done.

"For my own peace of mind–you're not going to kill me, are you? I don't have to worry about winding up in a ditch?"

Connor's hands flexed over the wheel. He shot her a dry look before turning back to the road. "I'm not a murderer."

Harper arched a brow. "That wasn't very convincing."

Connor let out a slow sigh. "I'm not going to hurt you. There's nothing to worry about. And why wait until now to ask that?"

Harper shrugged. "Didn't really think about it until we were stuck in this confined space and I realized I'm trapped with you for days." She exhaled, rubbing her temples. "And, well, I didn't have much of a choice."

Connor flicked her a glance, as if he wanted to ask more, but instead muttered, "Traffic's a nightmare. It's going to take forever to get out of the city."

Harper smirked. "What did you expect? The airlines are down. Everyone's scrambling to leave."

"I know," Connor grumbled. "Doesn't mean I can't be annoyed. A few-hour flight turned into a multi-day haul. I don't want to waste any more time."

"Well, once we're out of the city, we're stopping at the first gas station."

Connor turned to her, incredulous. "We're not stopping anytime soon."

Harper unfolded her arms. "In case you hadn't noticed, I'm soaked in coffee. I have to change. And find a bathroom."

Connor's eyes flicked to her shirt—visible proof of her

suffering. A weary breath escaped him as he shook his head. "You're not a toddler. You can hold it."

Harper stared at him, aghast. "I was going to go after security, but, in case you missed it, there was complete chaos, and I had exactly zero time between that and getting into this car. So, yeah. We're stopping."

Connor held her stare for a beat before exhaling sharply. "Fine. But after that, we're not stopping for a while."

Harper sank into the seat. "Great. Was that so hard?"

The car inched through bumper-to-bumper traffic, the sounds of the city fading behind them. As they merged onto the highway, the quiet became unbearable. Harper reached for the radio.

"What are you doing?" Connor asked, his voice carrying a warning.

"I can't take the silence. We need music."

"There's nothing wrong with silence. Better than filling it with nonsense."

"Well, that's nice for you, but a road trip calls for music." Harper cranked up her favorite country station, humming as the familiar tune filled the car.

Connor grimaced. "No. Absolutely not. We're not listening to country."

Harper scoffed. "You didn't care about music two seconds ago."

Connor twisted the dial to a 2000s rock station. "Driver picks the music. That's the rule."

Harper shot him a glare. "Okay, well, when do I get to drive?"

Connor shifted uncomfortably. "Are you a good driver?"

Harper gaped at him. "Yes. Are you?"

Connor said. "Never been in an accident. Never got a ticket."

Harper scoffed. "You must be an alien. Everyone's had at least one."

Connor's eyes narrowed. "You didn't answer the question."

She hesitated. "I'm a good driver. I've only gotten a couple of tickets. For speeding and talking on the phone."

Connor's expression didn't change. "And?"

She sighed. "I may have bumped into a parked car when I first started driving. And one time, a car stalled on the highway, and I hit them."

Connor gave her an unimpressed look.

"It was at night, and their lights were off. Not my fault. Even the cop agreed."

Connor exhaled. "I'm driving."

Harper's jaw dropped. "That's ridiculous. You'll burn yourself out and end up in your first accident."

Connor didn't argue. He simply inclined his head. "Fine. You can drive. But I'm driving most of the way, and at night."

Harper relaxed. "Works for me."

They settled into an uneasy stillness, well, uneasy for Harper, at least. Connor didn't seem to mind, but the way his fingers flexed around the steering wheel told her something deeper was eating at him. Tension radiated off him. He seemed to be a man stretched thin, right on the edge.

Not that he seemed to be the chatty type to begin with.

Harper was desperate for a distraction. She pulled out her phone and mindlessly scrolled through Instagram, thumbing past weekend brunches, reels, and travel shots. The usual.

A notification flashed across her screen—a message from the last person on earth she wanted to hear from.

Two

Day 1: The Road Trip Begins

Nate.

A cold trickle slid down her neck. It had been weeks since he stopped trying to contact her. Weeks of silence after months of feeling unsafe in her own city. Their breakup had been messy, and he hadn't made it easy to walk away. The texts. The calls. The showing up at her favorite spots. The promises that if Harper gave him another chance, things would be different.

And now, here he was again.

Hey. Thinking of you. Hope you're doing okay.

Harper's fingers hovered over the screen, thumb poised over the delete button, but it didn't move. Classic Nate. So casual, as if he hadn't spent so much time trying to manipulate her into coming back. She should delete it. She would delete it. But instead, she simply stared—caught between the instinct to shut him out and the gnawing curiosity of what he'd say next.

Connor's voice snapped her out of it.

"We should conserve our phones' batteries. I don't have a car charger, and I don't know when we'll be stopping to charge our phones."

Harper blinked, forcing herself into the present. Had he noticed her expression? Could he tell how rattled she was? She quickly locked her phone, shoving it into the cupholder. "Good point," she said, feigning normalcy. "Maybe we should stop at Target and grab a couple of chargers."

Connor shifted in his seat. "I'd rather not make unnecessary stops. We can charge our phones when we stop for the night."

Harper frowned. "Why are you hellbent on getting to California so fast? I get wanting to stay on schedule, but you do realize things aren't going to go perfectly, right?"

He gripped the steering wheel a bit tighter. "I need to get there. That's all."

Frustration bubbled up in Harper's chest. "Why are you going to California?"

Silence.

"You're really going to go this whole time without telling me anything about yourself?"

"There's nothing to tell."

He was determined to stay closed off, but Harper wasn't sure if it was stubbornness or something heavier. She knew enough to push him further, so she turned toward the window.

A gas station sign flashed by, and she sat up. "Oh! QuickChek at the next exit."

Connor barely spared it a glance. "I wanted to get more distance before stopping."

"Well, you're not the one soaked in coffee and dying for a bathroom break," she snapped. "A quick stop won't ruin your master plan."

Connor exhaled sharply but changed lanes anyway. They reached QuickChek within minutes, and he pulled the car up to the gas pump.

Harper glanced at the gas gauge as Connor started to get out of the car. "Aren't rentals supposed to be full when you pick them up?"

Connor looked annoyed at the question. "This one wasn't. I'd rather not make another stop anytime soon."

Harper nodded. Overly cautious, but fine. Before stepping out, she turned to him. "Pop the trunk?"

Without a word, he hit the latch. Harper grabbed her bag and headed toward the trunk, rifling through her suitcase until she pulled out a black hoodie. Good enough.

As she walked toward the store, she risked a glance over her shoulder. Connor stepped out and was filling up the car, standing still as he watched the numbers tick by on the pump. He shifted his weight to one side, his white t-shirt clinging to his frame. He looked... effortlessly put together–boots, jeans, and the kind of posture that exuded a sort of *don't mess with me* attitude. The type Harper was instantly attracted to.

She tore her eyes away. No.

In another life, maybe she'd flirt with him, test the waters. But Connor didn't look at her like that. He barely looked at her at all. He was single-minded, razor-focused on getting to California, and she was an inconvenience along for the ride.

And even if he was interested? Harper had no intention of going down that path, not after Nate. She wanted time alone, away from men, to figure out the rest of her life in peace.

Bracing herself, she stepped into the gas station, only to be met with a line of women waiting for the bathroom. Great.

Now she had no choice but to stand there, alone with her thoughts. She shifted her weight, glancing around, but the minutes dragged on. Finally, the door swung open, and it was her turn.

Harper peeled off her damp shirt, shivering as the cold air hit her skin. The stain wasn't worth salvaging, so she tossed the shirt in the garbage. She pulled on the black hoodie and exhaled as warmth settled around her. When she turned to the mirror, the sight made her stomach sink. No wonder Connor hadn't looked at her twice.

Harper's usually bright blue eyes were tired, smudged with mascara. The messy bun she had thrown her blonde hair in had devolved into disaster mode. She grabbed a paper towel, cleaned up her face, and swiped on emergency mascara—enough to look a little more like herself.

She did the rest of her business and left the bathroom, only to smack straight into Connor.

"Hey!" She stumbled back. "Oh. You."

He gave her a flat look. "You were taking a while."

She squared her shoulders. "There was a line. Lighten up."

He opened his mouth, but she breezed past him before he could get a word in. Petty? Maybe. But she didn't really care at this point.

Harper made a beeline for the snack aisle, scanning for road trip essentials.

A moment later, Connor was beside her. "What are you doing?"

She shot him a look. "Getting food. If we're not stopping anytime soon, I'd rather not starve."

Connor opened his mouth to argue, but stopped short, as he turned to grab a few things of his own.

Harper smiled as she grabbed her favorites: salt-and-vinegar chips, Reese's Pieces, chocolate donuts, and Vitamin Water. The good stuff.

When she met up with Connor near the register, she wasn't the least bit surprised by his selection: protein bars, beef sticks, water, and an energy drink.

She raised an eyebrow. "That's it? No fun snacks?"

Connor shook his head and handed his items to the cashier without saying a word.

As Harper waited for her turn, she looked around the gas station, her eyes drifting across the rows of mismatched shelves and buzzing coolers. Then, out of nowhere—

Connor laughed.

The sound caught Harper completely off guard. She turned in time to catch it–low and easy. The sharp edges of his expression softened into something unrecognizable, something almost… warm. The sight stopped her in her tracks. She wasn't sure what threw her more, the fact that he could look so relaxed, or how much she actually liked seeing him that way.

It was strange to see him this unguarded. Just a regular guy, not some brooding mystery. Maybe he wasn't always so serious. Maybe this was the side of him she hadn't seen yet.

She blinked as the cashier turned to her with a grin. "Alright, sweetheart, you ready?"

Harper jolted. "Oh–yeah, sorry." She fumbled with her items, still a little dazed. By the time she finished paying, Connor was already out the door and in the car.

Harper went straight to the driver's side and opened the door, only to find Connor sitting there fiddling with the GPS, irritation flickering across his face once more. "What are you doing?" he asked as she stood above him.

Harper replied. "You said you'd drive at night. So I'll drive now."

Connor sighed. "I can also drive during the day."

"Nope," she said chirped. "I want to listen to my music."

He looked exasperated. "Fine. But still no country. And watch out for stalled cars."

Harper said. "Oh, come on. One time. And it wasn't even my fault!"

Connor smirked as he begrudgingly got out and moved to the passenger seat. "Uh-huh. Sure."

Harper huffed, slid into the driver's seat and grabbed the wheel. The leather was warm. Her fingers flexed over the place where Connor's hands had been, and she forced herself to ignore the tiny jolt of awareness that ran up her arms. It was only body heat. Nothing more.

"Unbelievable." But despite herself, she felt a slight grin tug at her lips.

She adjusted the seat and mirrors before shooting him a sideways look. "Seriously, what is it with you and country music? It bothers you that much?"

Connor waited a beat. "It's not the music. Only... bad memories."

Harper looked toward him, intrigued. At last, he'd actually given her an honest answer. But she knew better than to push.

"Fair enough," she said simply. "That's all you had to say in the first place."

Connor gave her a sideways look. "No twenty questions?"

She shrugged. "I know how it is when something reminds you of things you'd rather not relive. I'm not about to pry."

A quick flicker crossed his face before he gave a grateful tilt of his head. "I appreciate that."

For a moment, the air between them felt… different. Lighter.

The GPS shattered the moment, jolting Harper. She glanced at the screen. "We've got a long stretch ahead on this highway."

Connor met her eyes and said, "No stops until Pennsylvania. Even then, quick."

Harper hummed in acknowledgment and pulled onto the highway, letting the rhythm of the road settle in.

Music filled the car. It was nostalgic, easy, the kind of songs you sang along to without thinking.

Out of the corner of her eye, she saw Connor staring out the window, lost in thought.

For now, she let the quiet stay.

Three

Day 1: An Unwelcome Surprise

T he city skyline melted into the sky behind them with the hum of the tires settling into a steady rhythm. They still had hours ahead, but Harper was determined to make good time. The early morning sun spilled through the windshield, casting a golden wash across the empty road.

Beside her, Connor unzipped his backpack and started rummaging through it, probably looking for headphones, a book, or something to occupy himself for the next stretch of highway. He didn't seem interested in talking, but Harper's curiosity won out.

A beat passed. "So… what do you actually do, when you're not being all mysterious and broody on cross-country road trips?"

He didn't answer.

She shot him a quick glance. "Seriously?"

Still nothing but the sound of zippers and fabric amid the low hum of tires on the road.

"I mean, I know you're not a magician or a spy," she went on, trying to keep it playful. "Unless that's your thing. In which case, I totally respect the code of silence."

Connor paused, his hand still inside the bag. "I work in medicine."

She blinked. "That's it? 'Medicine'? Like, Band-Aids or brain surgery?"

A pause. "Somewhere between," he said dryly.

Harper stared at him. "Wow. You're a vault."

"I'm tired," he muttered, clearly not interested in elaborating.

She swallowed her frustration, hands gripping the wheel a little harder. "Right. Of course. Heaven forbid we actually get to know each other a little bit while being trapped in a car for days."

That got him to open his eyes. He turned his head slowly, expression unreadable. "What do you want me to say?"

Harper turned her eyes to the road. "Nothing, apparently. I guess brooding is your love language."

The tension lingered, thick and unmoving.

His tone shifted, quieter now. "Talking doesn't mean connection, Harper."

She let out a dry laugh. "No, but it's usually how people start."

He didn't respond. Clearly, her sarcasm hadn't earned a reply.

Eventually, she gave up. The silence between them thickened, heavy with everything neither of them would say.

The hours had dragged on in suffocating silence. Neither Harper nor Connor had spoken much since their brief and forgettable exchange after they left the gas station in New York. Even the radio—once a potential escape—had lost its charm; cycling through the same tired hits every twenty minutes like some cruel loop. Harper's body ached from hours behind the wheel, even after Connor took over in the middle for a little while; her leg was stiff from pressing the gas, and her shoulders were stiff with tension.

Now, to top it off, her stomach had started to growl in protest—loud enough that she half-expected Connor to comment on it. She had finished every last snack she'd picked up from the gas station. They'd made just two brief stops to refuel, grab more gas-station snacks, and hit the bathroom. Connor had made it clear he wanted to keep moving.

Her eyes flicked to the dashboard clock: 3:17 p.m. They switched seats at the last gas station, and Harper had been driving for the last several hours. The sky was starting to change as they went through Pennsylvania, the signs of the late afternoon sun slanting across the highway in golden streaks.

She shifted in her seat, her patience thinning by the minute. Hunger twisted in her stomach as her hands closed more firmly on the wheel.

Harper spotted a sign ahead for food. Without hesitation, she flicked on her blinker and veered off the highway, the exit approaching fast.

Beside her, Connor tensed, his posture stiffening. "What are you doing?"

"I'm stopping for food," she replied simply, focusing on the road ahead.

Connor's eyes flicked to her before returning to the road. "No. We can't stop now."

Harper shot him a look. "Why not? We've been driving for hours. We should eat, stretch, and refuel."

He scanned the gas gauge, calculating the distance. "There's enough to make it a couple more hours. No reason to stop yet."

Harper didn't break her gaze. "Well, I'm driving, and I say we're stopping."

Connor huffed, eyes narrowing, but didn't protest further.

She ignored the stiffness in his shoulders, her stomach a louder voice than his resistance. The exit led them through the town of Claysville, and Harper spotted the neon glow of a Starlight Diner. It was a sign, literally. She pulled into the lot with a relieved sigh and cut the engine, her body grateful for the break.

As soon as Harper stepped out of the car, she stretched her arms high above her head, groaning softly as her spine cracked. She rolled her shoulders, the muscles taut from hours of sitting. She found a low metal railing near the entrance and propped one foot up, leaning into a deep calf stretch as the late-day heat clung to her skin.

Connor stalked a few steps ahead, his expression hard, strides clipped. He didn't look at her as he muttered, "Let's get this over with."

Harper blinked, lowering her leg. "Seriously? We've been crammed in that car for hours, and you won't even let me breathe for two minutes?"

He stopped short and turned to face her, crossing his arms in front of him.

Harper stared at him, exhaling sharply as she threw her arms wide. "You're the *worst* road trip partner. You know that?"

For a fraction of a second, barely there, his lips twitched. Not quite a smile, but close enough to make her blink.

Harper narrowed her eyes, pointing at him. "Was that a smile?"

Connor's face immediately shuttered, as if someone had flipped a switch. "No," he said flatly. "I was thinking about how ridiculous you look now."

Harper scoffed, her moment of triumph deflated. Rolling her eyes, she turned toward the diner's entrance, Connor's long strides easily outpacing her as he reached the door first.

To her surprise, he held it open for her.

Harper froze for a moment, her eyes flicking up to him, thrown off by the unexpected gesture. She blinked, caught off guard. "Uh... thanks."

Connor gave her an unreadable look, his tone surprisingly soft. "You're welcome."

They entered the diner, and Harper was immediately greeted by the smell of fresh coffee, sizzling burgers, and warm, greasy comfort food. For the first time all day, Harper's shoulders loosened a notch. It was a stupid thing, but the clatter of forks and soft hum of an old jukebox felt almost... normal. As they walked further in, she turned to Connor. "I'm gonna hit the bathroom. Can you grab us a table?"

He nodded without protest and made his way toward the hostess stand. Harper took a moment to weave her way through the booths, passing clusters of locals and a few other travelers, her mind drifting from the endless road to the mundane task of finding a restroom.

She spotted the sign at the back when a voice sliced through the air.

"Harper?"

Cold washed over her. Her breath caught. Every muscle in her body locked into place.

No. Not here. Not him.

That voice was smooth, familiar, and laced with something she didn't want to name. It curled around her like a vice, squeezing the air from her lungs. A slow, involuntary shiver crawled down her spine as her pulse pounded in her chest.

Her feet felt rooted to the floor, but somehow, she turned.

And there he was.

She felt her heart drop, a sickening reminder of everything she thought she'd left behind.

Nate.

He looked the same as ever. Crisp suit, clean-shaven except for the faintest trace of a five o'clock shadow. His blond hair was perfectly styled, the kind of flawless grooming that always made Harper feel second-rate. His piercing blue eyes locked onto hers—sharp, calculating, sizing up the situation before making his next move. A confident smile spread across his face as he strode toward her, each step more certain than the last.

Harper's breath hitched. Instinctively, she took a step back, her mind racing. "What the hell are you doing here?"

Nate raised an eyebrow, feigning surprise. "I'm here on business." He gestured toward a man in a nearby booth—rough around the edges, the kind of guy who'd clearly made a lot of bad choices. Nate turned to her, smooth as ever. "Did you get my text?"

Her fists clenched, jaw locking as she fought the sting behind her eyes. "I did."

Nate tilted his head slightly, his voice smooth—almost too casual. "And?" he pressed, the words dripping with an edge of entitlement. "Why didn't you respond? I wanted to make sure you were okay. It's been a while."

Her stomach churned, a tight knot forming in her gut. Nate was always this way—slipping past boundaries, testing her patience, acting as if he still had some claim on her.

"We broke up months ago," she snapped, her voice sharp, biting. "In case you forgot, when people break up, they don't stay in touch."

Nate stepped closer, closing the distance between them, his cologne flooding her senses with unwelcome memories. "Come on, Harper. You always came back before. Don't pretend you weren't thinking about it."

His proximity was suffocating, and now, Harper could see the subtle tension in his jaw, the flicker of something unreadable in his eyes. Her heart raced, and her skin crawled.

"I don't know what part of 'I'm done' you don't understand," she said, her voice low and steady. "We're not getting together again. Don't contact me. Ever."

Her body stiffened, bracing for him to push further. When he didn't say anything, she turned to leave.

But before she could take a step, Nate's hand shot out, gripping her arm with a force that made her freeze.

Her breath caught in her throat, the familiar cold rush of panic rising within her as he smiled smugly, his fingers firm but controlled. "You know it's only a matter of time before you come around."

Harper's pulse raced as she yanked her arm, but his grip held fast. "Let go of me."

A voice rang out, cutting through the tension like a blade.

"Let her go."

The words weren't loud, but they carried enough weight to make both of them turn.

Connor was standing a few feet away, his arms loose at his sides, but the tension in his posture was undeniable. His six-foot-something frame towered over Nate, and his eyes were cold, intensely focused.

Nate hesitated, he dropped his hand as he looked from Connor to Harper. His lips curled into a brief, sardonic smile, though it didn't reach his eyes. "Who's this?" he asked, looking between them. "Already got yourself a new boyfriend?"

Harper didn't hesitate. She moved closer to Connor, her protective instinct flaring up. "He's not my boyfriend."

Connor stepped toward Nate, his presence imposing. "Doesn't matter what we are. You're not touching her that way again."

The air between the two men crackled, heavy with the promise of conflict. Neither one blinked as their eyes were locked in a quiet standoff.

Nate scoffed, clearly amused. "Relax, man. We're only talking."

Connor took a step closer, his expression unreadable. "Then you won't mind giving her some space."

There was a tense beat, the air tight between them.

A few heads turned from nearby tables, the strain between the two of them growing noticeable. Nate, constantly aware of his image, seemed to catch the shift in the air. He smoothed his suit and faced Harper again.

"I'm sorry," he said, though the apology rang hollow. "I shouldn't have done that."

Harper crossed her arms, the frustration rising. "Bullshit."

Nate's smug smile returned, but it was tighter now, tinged with irritation. "Enjoy your meal," he said, flicking a calculated glance at Connor before turning on his heel and striding toward his booth.

Harper exhaled sharply, the knot inside her beginning to loosen. Her entire body was on edge; shoulders tense, fists clenched. Damn him. He always had a way of making her feel cornered, even after everything.

Connor's voice brought her out of the fog, gentle but steady.

"You okay?"

Harper blinked, realizing she hadn't processed what he said. She shook her head slightly, trying to clear the fog from her thoughts. "Sorry, what?"

Connor's eyes softened a fraction, his concern clear in his gaze. "Go to the bathroom. I'll stay out here."

She stalled for a moment, but the understanding in his eyes was enough to make her nod. "Thanks."

Connor gave a nod in return, his presence a silent promise of support as she pushed through the door marked "Women."

The moment she was alone, everything crashed down on her in an instant.

Her breath hitched, and a wave of heat washed over her, only to be followed by a biting chill. She gripped the sink, her knuckles white as she stared at her reflection—pale, wide-eyed, unsteady. She looked shaken. Worse, she felt it. It shouldn't have hit so hard to see Nate after all these months. But it did. Everything she'd tried to bury surged to the surface, and all the old memories were impossible to ignore.

She turned the faucet on, soaked a paper towel, and pressed it to her face and neck. The coolness soothed her, and her heartbeat gradually slowed, her hands steadying.

Once she felt steady enough to face the world, she took a deep breath and stepped out of the bathroom.

Connor was still there.

"He and his friend left," he said, glancing at her with a practiced calmness.

Relief flooded through Harper, and she let out a slow breath. "Thank God. I don't think I could've stayed if he hadn't."

Connor gave a simple nod. "C'mon. Our table's over here."

Harper followed him, grateful that she wasn't alone at this

moment.

Four

Day 1: One Room, One Bed

As they made their way through the diner, Harper's eyes drifted to the booth where Connor had been sitting earlier. It was tucked in the far corner, almost hidden, but with a clear, uninterrupted view of the back and the exact spot where she and Nate had stood moments before.

When they sat down, a waitress appeared beside the table, all sunshine and a practiced cheer. "Well, aren't you two cute," she said with a grin as she handed them menus. "I'll give you a minute to look, but let me know if this is a special occasion—anniversary or a little date?"

Harper blinked, caught off guard.

Connor let out a low, awkward chuckle and said, "Uh… a stop along the way."

The waitress winked. "Got it. I'll grab you two some waters to start."

She disappeared before Harper could say anything else.

Harper stared down at her menu but didn't really see it. A flush had crept into her cheeks that had nothing to do with the summer heat outside.

Connor didn't say anything, but when Harper glanced up, she caught the faintest curve of a smirk tugging at the corner of his mouth.

"What?" she asked, bracing herself.

"Nothing," he said quickly, but the amusement in his eyes was unmistakable.

Harper rolled her eyes and muttered, "She probably says that to everyone."

Connor continued to look at his menu, that half-smile still hovering. "Probably."

Before she could come up with a response, the moment was broken by the return of her thoughts to Nate. Her fingers curled slightly on the table, and the playful heat faded into something cold.

Connor's voice broke through her memories, grounding her. "You okay?"

Harper looked into his eyes, his concern so clear it nearly disarmed her. She took a slow breath, forcing herself to relax. "No. Not really." She exhaled sharply before adding, "But I really appreciate what you did back there. That meant more than you know."

Connor watched her carefully and asked, "Is that the reason why you're going to California?"

Harper paused for a beat, already knowing he'd put it together. "Partly. Well, yes. Pretty much the entire reason."

Her fingers drummed lightly on the edge of the table as she hesitated, unsure of how much to say. Something about the way Connor was looking at her made her continue. "That was

Nate. My ex-boyfriend. I broke up with him a few months ago."

Connor raised an eyebrow, his expression softening with understanding. "Didn't end well, I take it?"

Harper let out a dry, humorless laugh. "Not exactly. He's used to getting what he wants, and he didn't like it when I told him I was done."

Connor's expression darkened slightly. "Did he hurt you?"

The question hit harder than expected. Harper paused before answering, her voice low but steady. "That was the first time he ever put his hand on me."

Connor's gaze remained steady. There was no pity in his eyes, only an understanding that made her feel she wasn't alone in this. She continued, her voice softening. "We dated in college, broke up, and then reconnected a few years later. I thought he was the one. But… he wasn't. Over time, it became clear—just as everyone else had seen—that he wasn't who I believed him to be."

Harper's voice faltered, breath hitching as she stared past Connor, her gaze fixed on something only she could see. "Like I said, he never hit me, but… there were other things." She paused, swallowing hard. Her fingers curled around the table's edge, knuckles white.

"The way he spoke to me—it chipped away at who I was. At first, I thought I was imagining it. That I was too sensitive." Her laugh came out brittle, barely there. "But it got worse. Constant criticism, twisting my words, making me doubt myself."

She blinked fast, willing the heat behind her eyes to retreat. "It took me months to walk away. And even then, he didn't stop. The calls, the texts… showing up when I least expected it."

Harper realized her fingers were gripping the edge of the table and forced herself to loosen them. She felt exposed in a raw way, but Connor didn't seem uncomfortable. He didn't interrupt, didn't fidget. He just sat with it, eyes steady on hers like he wasn't going anywhere.

Before she could say more, the waitress returned with their drinks. "You two ready to order?"

Harper scrambled to order the first thing she saw. "Uh, buffalo burger, please."

Connor nodded with ease. "Bacon burger."

The waitress left, and the weight of the conversation settled over them again. Harper took a slow breath, trying to pull herself together. She hadn't expected to talk about all of this, but somehow, with Connor, it felt safe, as if she was shedding the burden she'd been carrying.

The earlier moment had stalled when the waitress came to take their order, but Connor picked up the thread, leaning against the booth. "Took a lot of guts for you to leave," he said, his voice calm but edged. "He's clearly not the type who can handle losing control."

Harper mirrored his position, sinking deeper into the seat with a dry laugh. "That's one way of putting it."

Connor studied her for a moment. "I can see why you insisted on sharing a car."

She smiled slightly. "I know I can be a pain. Sorry about that. But if I'd stayed in New York another day…" She trailed off, unwilling to put words to the rest.

Connor's fingers tapped quietly on the table, taking in her words. He leaned in just a little, a subtle change in his posture. After a moment, he spoke again. "I'm heading to California for my dad's funeral."

Harper blinked, caught off guard. She hadn't expected him to share so openly.

She said nothing, giving him space. A moment passed. "We had a falling out a few years ago. Last week… out of nowhere, he died in a car accident."

Harper's instinct was to reach out, her fingers brushing his forearm lightly. "I'm so sorry," she whispered.

Connor let her hand linger for a second before pulling away, his eyes turning down, distant. "My family held off on the funeral until my sister could return from Europe."

Harper nodded, processing his words. "I get it. You should be there."

A heavy silence stretched between them before she finally spoke. "Were you close? Before the fallout?"

Connor's jaw tensed, his eyes darkening. "Yeah. We were. Very close."

He seemed to want to say more, but the waitress returned with their food, and the moment slipped away.

They didn't talk during their meal, Harper glancing at him occasionally, but he was focused on his burger, clearly not in the mood to share more. She took the hint and didn't press.

When the check came, Connor handed over his credit card before she had a chance to reach for hers.

Harper frowned. "Hey, I was gonna pay for mine. I'm not a moocher."

Connor shook his head. "You can get the next one."

She said, "Fine. But seriously, don't try to pay for it."

He smirked slightly. "Wouldn't dream of it."

After one last stop at the bathroom, they headed to the car. This time, Connor slid into the driver's seat without a word. Harper didn't argue; her leg still ached, and honestly, she didn't have the energy to fight for the wheel.

As the miles rolled by, the energy in the car was noticeably lighter. It was worlds better than when they'd first set out. Harper stared out the window, watching the trees go by, and decided not to push for conversation. She could tell that Connor wasn't the type to fill the space with small talk. If he wanted to talk, he would. If not, she would let it be.

For now, they were two people on the road, headed in separate directions but sharing the same journey.

The fading light outside transformed the world into muted shades of blue and gray, the sky softening as dusk settled in. The desolate road stretched ahead, broken only by the flash of a streetlight or the distant silhouette of a lone farm silo. Harper shifted in her seat, the steady hum of the engine filling the void, broken only by the sporadic buzz of Connor's phone on the console between them. Every time it lit up, the same name flashed across the screen—Allison.

Harper tried not to glance at her own phone, but the boredom from being in the car pressed in on her with a heavy, suffocating weight. It felt as though they'd been driving forever, the miles stretching endlessly before them. Her thumb moved in a mindless rhythm, scrolling through the same apps, checking the time, checking the news. Anything to fill the space.

Before she realized it, she'd been scrolling far more than she meant to. Harper's thumb froze when a low battery notification flashed across the screen, the bright text sharp and clear over the darkening background.

"Shit," she muttered under her breath, annoyed at herself.

Connor's eyes flicked to her from the road, his brow furrowing. "What?"

"My phone's about to die," she said, frustration creeping into her voice. "We should probably stop soon."

Without hesitation, he shook his head. "No. Not yet. I want

to get far into Indiana before we stop."

Harper glanced over at the gas gauge. It was dipping below a quarter tank. "We'll need to stop soon anyway. I'm pretty sure your phone's almost out of battery, too."

Connor kept his eyes on the road. "I'm driving until we're almost empty. We'll stop after that."

Harper gave him a pointed look. "You don't strike me as the type to let the gas get that low."

"I'm normally not," he said, the edge of impatience in his voice. "But I want to make up time before we're delayed even more."

She raised an eyebrow. "You know it'll take the same amount of time whether we stop now or in an hour, right?"

Connor shot her a sharp glance, irritation flickering across his face.

"I'm just saying," Harper added, shrugging. "You can't control time no matter how hard you try."

The moment stretched on, broken only by the hum of tires and a low, steady song on the radio. Bored, Harper snuck a look at Connor's phone resting between them on the console, the screen lighting up enough for the same name to flash.

Allison. Three dots. *Are you seriously still not answering me?*

Harper's brows lifted. Another message buzzed in seconds. *Call me. Please.*

Harper didn't say anything at first. She leaned into the seat and stared out the window, though the questions were already gnawing at her.

She debated whether to ask, but something about Connor's posture made her hesitate. Whoever Allison was, she was either important or unwelcome—maybe both. Instead, Harper continued to watch the headlights stretch ahead of them. "You know, if you're trying to drain your battery, you're doing a great job."

Connor let out an exasperated sigh, grabbed the phone, and stuffed it into his pocket.

Harper scoffed. "Oh, come on. You're really mad about that?"

"I don't like snoops," he said, flatly.

Harper sat up straighter, eyes wide with feigned innocence. "Hard not to, considering it's the only thing making noise for the past few hours. Maybe if you didn't angle it like a billboard—"

Before she could say anything else, Connor spoke up. "We'll stop at the next exit, get gas, and find somewhere to sleep."

Harper's eyebrows rose in surprise. "Oh. Great. Glad to see you still have a small sense of sanity."

Connor ignored her comment, pulling off an exit outside Prairie City, close to the edge of Indiana. The gas station they found sat still and dimly lit, tucked off a nearly deserted stretch of road. When he parked, Harper unbuckled her seatbelt. "This one's mine," she said, heading for the pump.

He gave her a nod as she stepped out of the car and slid her card into the pump. The night air felt heavier than it should have. Overhead, one of the gas station lights flickered, casting an unsteady glow across the empty lot.

Harper shifted on her feet and scanned the lot out of habit. Then froze.

A sleek black car glided into one of the distant spaces, its windows so darkly tinted that even in broad daylight, no one could see inside. Whoever was in there didn't get out, and the stillness of it sent an uneasy ripple through Harper.

She tried to brush it off. It was a late traveler. That's all.

But her hold on the pump grew firmer anyway.

Ever since Nate showed up, everything felt a little darker. And the idea that anyone could be behind that glass and watching her made Harper's skin crawl.

She told herself not to overthink it. Maybe whoever was in the black car was waiting for someone or checking directions. Still, her gut churned, and her unease lingered.

As she finished filling the tank and climbed into the car, Connor was wrapping up a message. She didn't mention it, though she couldn't help but wonder who Allison was.

He pocketed the phone without a word and pulled out of the station, merging onto the road. Harper checked the rearview mirror, spotting the black car pulling out behind them.

She kept an eye on it for a few moments before it turned onto a side road.

She exhaled, trying to calm herself. Nothing to worry about.

They continued driving until they reached a small roadside motel, the kind that didn't promise much beyond a bed for the night. It didn't matter to Harper; she only wanted to sleep. And definitely a place to charge her phone.

Connor pulled into the parking lot and climbed out without a word. He popped the trunk, took out his suitcase and backpack, and left Harper to get her own. The muggy June air hit her the second she stepped out, thick and heavy. Sweat clung to the nape of her neck as she hauled her bag from the trunk. Once she shut it, Connor slipped the keys into his pocket and headed toward the building marked *Front Office*.

Harper followed, fatigue weighing heavily on her steps. Inside the motel, a bored teenager was at the desk, not bothering to lift his head as they walked in.

Connor rapped his knuckles on the desk. The teen reluctantly looked up. "Can I help you?"

"Two rooms, please."

The teen shook his head, unimpressed. "Only got one left."

Connor's eyebrows shot up. "You're kidding. It's that busy?"

The kid shrugged, uninterested.

Connor turned to Harper. "Want to find another place?"

She paused. Connor didn't seem the type to try anything, especially with her, and after the day she'd had, she didn't have the brainpower to think beyond passing out. "It's fine. All I care about is getting some rest."

Connor nodded before turning toward the teen. "We'll take it."

"You have a credit card?"

Before Connor could reach for his wallet, Harper slid her card across the counter.

Connor shot her a look. "I was going to pay."

Harper waved him off. "Relax. There'll be plenty of other things to pay for."

He muttered, "Thanks."

"You're welcome."

They finished up and headed to room 13. The motel was a single-story, wrap-around structure, the kind of place where the doors opened directly into the parking lot. Harper unlocked the door, feeling an odd flicker of nostalgia at using a physical key instead of a keycard.

The door creaked open, and her stomach dropped to her feet. One bed. Behind her, Connor stepped inside, his presence suddenly too close, too real. A thought slipped in before she could stop it—could she really trust him? The question irritated her. Of course she could. Probably.

Unease wound through her, but she forced a casual tone. "Well, that's inconvenient."

Five

Day 1: Nighttime

She had been expecting there to be two beds in the room; her brain hadn't quite wrapped around the fact that they might be sharing a bed.

Connor, on the other hand, barely reacted. He strode in, left his suitcase near one of the sad-looking chairs, and dropped his backpack at the foot of the bed, from where he immediately pulled out his phone charger. Harper lingered near the door, glancing around. The room was as uninspired as every cheap motel; neutral colors, generic furniture, a space designed to be forgotten.

With a sigh, Harper stepped inside and dropped her bags near the far side of the bed. She dug through rumpled clothes and tangled cords in search of her charger. For a moment, her heart ticked faster when she couldn't find it.

Her fingers caught the familiar cord, tangled beneath a shirt. Relief rose as she freed it and plugged it into the outlet beside the desk. Harper's phone buzzed to life, the screen glowing in the dim room.

She waited a minute before opening her messages, bracing herself for a name she didn't want to see.

Nothing from Nate.

She let out a breath she hadn't realized she was holding.

Good.

Sliding into the chair by the desk, she took a few minutes to reply to messages—mainly updates to her friend, Sydney, in California, letting her know where they were, just in case. Her fingers moved quickly, but her gaze kept drifting toward Connor.

He was sitting at the edge of the bed, staring at his phone screen.

Harper pushed to her feet. "I'm going to take a shower," she said.

Connor barely looked up. "Um. Okay?"

She stepped closer. "Can I have the car keys?"

His eyes flicked up, confused. "Why?"

Harper held out her hand. "Because I don't want you taking off while I'm in the shower."

Connor gawked at her. "Are you serious?"

"Dead serious. We don't really know each other, and if you leave me stranded, I'll almost certainly be assaulted in a place like this."

Connor ran a hand down his face, exasperated. "I would never leave you stranded."

"Well, clearly I've only made your life miserable so far on this trip, so I'm protecting myself in case you decide I'm too much."

He shook his head, frustration clear as he dug into his pocket for the keys. Before handing them over, he said, "If we're doing this, I'm taking the keys when I shower."

Harper met his eyes, unwavering. "Obviously."

He dropped the keys into her hand, and she turned to gather her things. When she glanced over her shoulder, Connor was once more lost in his phone.

The shower was heaven as the hot water washed away hours on the road. By the time she finished brushing her teeth and changed into her sleepwear—red plaid shorts and a plain black tee—she felt a little more human.

She stepped out of the bathroom, towel-drying her damp hair. Connor looked up from the bed, his mouth parting slightly as if he was going to say something.

Harper narrowed her eyes. "What? I didn't take that long."

Connor paused and shook his head. "I wasn't going to say that. It's just—" He stopped short.

She arched a brow. "Just what?"

He exhaled. "Can I have the keys? I'm taking a shower."

Harper eyed him curiously, but handed over the keys without saying anything.

He grabbed a pile of clothes and his toothbrush before disappearing into the bathroom. As the water turned on, Harper sat on the bed, reaching for her phone. Connor's phone was nearby, screen dark, tempting.

She never snooped. Ever.

But Allison's name hovered at the edge of her thoughts.

She clenched her jaw and turned away, grabbing a towel from the closet to lay over her pillow so her wet hair wouldn't soak into it. Glancing around the room, Harper figured Connor wouldn't mind if she turned out the lights, except for the small one near his side of the bed. The calm of darkness immediately relaxed her. She slid beneath the covers and curled up at the farthest edge of the bed, careful to leave plenty of space between them.

Because if the idea of sharing a bed with him made her this aware of every inch between them now, she could only imagine how awkward it'd be when he climbed in.

Harper thought exhaustion would knock her out, but her mind wouldn't stop racing. She barely noticed when the shower shut off, and the bathroom door opened. She told herself not to look, and she listened as Connor set down his things, checked his phone, and turned off the light before pulling the sheet aside to climb in. When he tugged at the comforter, she felt it slip from her grip.

She rolled over enough to grumble, "Hey. Don't hog the blanket."

In the dim light of the moon peeking through the drapes, she could make out the annoyed look on his face.

"I wouldn't have to pull it if you weren't holding onto it as if your life depended on it," he muttered.

Harper scoffed. "I'm trying to stay far away from you. Wouldn't want to touch you accidentally and you burst into flames."

Connor sighed. "Relax. We're adults. We have to share this bed, and yeah, we're probably going to bump into each other. It's not the end of the world." He shifted, settling in. "If you want some of the blanket, you'll have to move closer."

Harper huffed but scooted slightly toward the middle. The warmth of his body heat made her hyper-aware of how close they were. As she shifted once more, her hand lightly grazed his skin.

She jolted. "Are you not wearing a shirt?"

Connor's voice was low, maybe even slightly amused. "I'm

not. This is how I sleep. Problem?"

"No," she said quickly. "I… wasn't expecting it."

Turning away, she pulled more of the blanket around her, trying to avoid touching his legs, which were way too close. She felt him mirror her movement, settling back to back with her. In a quiet truce, Harper drifted into a deep sleep.

Only seconds seemed to pass before something jolted Harper awake. Disoriented, she blinked into the darkness. The room was silent, so why was she awake?

A sudden warmth grounded her. Connor's arms wrapped around her.

She flinched, breaking free from his arms and jumping out of the bed, as her heart thundered within her, the frantic rhythm loud in the silence. Her hand instinctively rested over her heart, seeking calm.

As her eyes adjusted to the darkness, his figure became clearer, every detail sharper in the dim light. His features were relaxed, his expression softer than she was used to—none of the usual guarded edge or sharpness in his jaw. Asleep, he looked… peaceful. Almost gentle.

Harper took a steadying breath and told herself to get a grip; they were both sleeping. She climbed into the bed and shifted as far away as she could, praying it wouldn't happen again.

As she was about to drift off, a noise at the door made her freeze.

At first, she thought she had imagined it. She sat up, straining to listen.

Silence.

A knock.

Harper's breath caught. She slipped out of bed and crept to the door, standing on her toes to peer through the peephole.

Her chest tightened.

A greasy-looking man stood at the door—Nate's friend from the diner.

Harper clamped a hand over her mouth to stifle her gasp. *Why the hell was he here?* The man shifted as he looked up and down the hallway before knocking once more, louder this time.

She spun and rushed to the bed, shaking Connor's shoulder. "Connor! Wake up!"

He groggily muttered, "What… what's going on?"

"Someone's at the door."

That woke him up fast. His body went rigid as he sat up, instantly alert. "Did you see who it was?"

Harper swallowed hard. "The guy from the diner. The one with Nate."

Even in the dark, she could feel Connor's whole body tense. He swung his legs over the bed and strode to the door, shooting her a look.

"Stay behind me."

Harper nodded and pressed close to his back as he checked the peephole. He unlocked the door and cracked it open enough to speak.

"What the hell do you want?" Connor's voice was low, dangerous.

Harper strained to hear the response, but it was too muffled. She saw Connor take something from the man before he growled, "Stay the fuck away from us, or it won't end well for you."

He slammed the door shut and locked it.

Harper's pulse pounded. "What did he want?"

Connor didn't answer right away. He walked to his nightstand, flicked on the light, and turned to face her—black gym shorts hanging low on his hips, his toned chest catching the warm glow. Harper's eyes flicked to a small package in his hands.

Connor gave it to her. "He said this was for you."

Confused, Harper took it. The package was light, and her name was scrawled across the top, in Nate's handwriting.

A sick feeling coiled in her stomach.

Her hands trembled as she tore it open. Inside was a bracelet.

Her bracelet.

The one Nate had given her on Valentine's Day when they got back together after breaking up the first time. The one she'd left behind at his apartment, not wanting to carry any memories of him.

Harper's breath caught as she fumbled inside the package and pulled out a folded note. Dread pooled in her gut as she read the words.

"I wanted you to remember what we had. I'll always be around."

The bracelet and note slipped from her fingers.

Panic slammed into her. Her breath came fast and shallow.

Connor was in front of her in a flash, his hands steady on her shoulders as he guided her down onto the edge of the bed. "Sit," he said, his voice firm.

He crouched in front of her, tipping her chin up until their eyes met. "Harper. What did the note say?"

She couldn't get the words out. All she could do was point toward the crumpled paper on the floor.

Connor picked it up, his eyes scanning the scribbled message. His jaw locked. The muscles in his face clenched as he crushed the note in his fist, the paper crackling beneath his grip.

"He knows where you are," he said, his voice low, controlled, and dangerous. Rage flickered beneath the surface.

She forced the words out. "Looks like it."

Connor began to pace, running a hand through his hair. "How the hell did he find us?" His mind moved faster than his steps. "Maybe he followed us from the diner."

Cold sweat swept up and down her spine. Her mind flashed to the sleek black car at the gas station—the one that hadn't moved until they left. She hadn't seen who was inside, but the memory turned her blood cold.

Connor moved to the window, carefully shifting one slat of the blinds with his finger. He scanned the parking lot, his jaw tight. "We need to leave. Now."

Harper didn't move. "Wait… shouldn't we call someone? The police?"

He turned to her slowly, his expression unreadable. "And tell them what? That a guy gave you a bracelet and looked suspicious? No threat. No proof. The police won't care."

She looked down, her hands slightly shaking in her lap. Connor stepped in closer, his voice gentle. "If you want to call, we will. If it makes you feel safer."

Harper glanced between him and the bracelet lying on the ground, coiled and waiting—a snake ready to strike.

"No," she said softly. "You're right. Let's go."

Within minutes, they were packed. Connor pulled on a shirt, socks, and shoes, while Harper stepped into her sneakers, her eyes flicking to the bracelet and crumpled note. She gave them a fleeting glance but didn't reach for them. The thought of bringing them with her made her want to hurl.

They slipped out of the room and hurried down the hallway, Harper's heart thudding in time with their footsteps. At the front desk, the same half-asleep teenager was still slouched behind the counter, bathed in the glow of a flickering screen.

Connor stepped up, placing both hands on the counter with finality. "The guy who walked in," he said, voice low and cold. "What did he want?"

The teen straightened instantly, eyes wide. "He said he was a friend. Asked what room you were in."

Connor's jaw tensed. "A friend," he repeated, his voice cold and sharp. "At three in the morning?"

The teen's mouth opened and closed, but no defense came out.

"That didn't raise any red flags?" Connor asked, the words razor-sharp.

"I–I didn't think–he looked normal," the kid stammered.

Connor leaned in slightly, his tone dropping into something more dangerous. "He looked normal?"

The teen paled.

"Forget it," Connor snapped, pushing off the counter. "You're giving us a refund."

The kid nearly fell over himself trying to comply, his fingers shaking as he typed. "Okay—it's done."

Connor offered a brief nod. "Good."

Without another word, he turned on his heel, and Harper quickly fell into step behind him.

Her eyes darted around the dark parking lot feeling as if every shadow felt suspect, every parked car a potential threat.

She didn't say a word when Connor headed for the driver's side. He unlocked the car and popped the trunk, their suitcases and bags thudding into it a moment later. They slammed their doors in near-unison, the car sealing them into a cocoon of adrenaline and fear.

The engine roared to life, but neither of them spoke.

Connor reversed fluidly, tires screeching as he peeled out of the parking lot. Harper sank into the seat, her grip tightening on the armrest as he sped through the empty streets, weaving between shadows cast by flickering streetlights. She knew better than to say anything at that moment. Connor's mood was razor-sharp, his grip on the wheel white-knuckled.

Harper couldn't stand to look at Connor or the streets ahead, so instead she stared out the window, scanning the darkness. She had a sick feeling twisting in her gut—the kind that whispered she wasn't paranoid at the gas station, that she hadn't imagined anything. If she ever spotted that sleek, familiar car, she was certain whose hands would be on the wheel.

Connor kept veering onto side roads, cutting through dimly lit neighborhoods and empty intersections, his eyes flicking to the rearview mirror more often than they should. He was testing the waters, seeing if they had a tail. Harper swallowed hard.

By the time they hit the highway, she peeked at the dashboard clock: 4:00 a.m. The night clung stubbornly to the horizon, though the first hints of dawn lurked at the edges of the sky. Connor exhaled through his nose. For a second, he said nothing, his fingers flexing on the wheel, tightening, loosening. When he spoke, his voice came out tense.

"I can't believe this."

Harper's body tensed all at once.

Connor went on. "I knew this trip was cursed from the start."

She turned to look at him. "You can't believe this? Who's the one being stalked?"

Connor kept looking ahead, the muscle in his jaw twitching. "Are there any other ex-boyfriends I should be aware of? Or is this trip a reunion tour where every stop comes with a new asshole trying to fuck things up?"

Harper's head snapped toward him, disbelief flashing through her. "Are you seriously making this about you?"

Connor's hands clenched the wheel. "Yeah, I am, actually. Because this is turning into the trip from hell. I should've said 'fuck it' and gone to another car rental place. Then I wouldn't be stuck wondering if a psycho is following us."

Harper let out a sharp, humorless laugh. "Oh, I'm so sorry this is inconvenient for you. You don't think this is worse for me? I left that jackass, and now I have to worry about seeing him again. Even in California, when I'm trying to put as much distance between us as possible."

Connor didn't answer. He kept his hands locked on the wheel, staring straight ahead.

Harper crossed her arms and sank into her seat, her pulse drumming beneath her skin. The space between them felt suffocating, thick with unspoken words, and barely contained anger. She turned towards the window, focusing on the road signs and the darkened countryside, trying to think about anything other than the infuriating man next to her.

Six

Day 2: Disruption

Time dragged on as the sky shifted from deep midnight to a pale, washed-out yellow. Harper had expected exhaustion to kick in, to offer some kind of peaceful slumber, but the lingering unease from the night's scare kept her wired, her mind looping through worst-case scenarios.

She risked a glance at Connor. He hadn't relaxed an inch. His expression hardened while his hands steadied on the wheel. The bad mood from earlier still clung to him. Harper wasn't looking forward to another round of *This Is All Your Fault* commentary. But no matter how much she tried to push it away, her stomach twisted at the thought of Nate and his slimy friend tracking them down. The paranoia prickled at her skin.

Unable to stop herself, she turned, scanning the cars behind them, half-expecting to see Nate's face lurking in the sea of headlights.

She caught Connor watching her from the corner of his eye.

Harper bristled, covering nerves with irritation. "What?" she snapped. "Can I not glance around?"

Connor didn't take the bait. He shook his head, voice flat. "I know what you're looking for. But I'm not going down that road."

As they neared Powellville in Missouri, the road ahead thickened with red brake lights. Harper groaned, shifting forward to get a better look. The GPS confirmed the bad news—two hours of standstill traffic due to an accident.

Connor muttered something under his breath, running a hand through his messy hair before resting his elbow on the window.

"I can drive," Harper offered, her voice softer now. "If you want to try and get some sleep."

Connor looked over, exhaustion pulling at the edges of his sharp features, but he shook his head. "Thanks. But I'm good."

They sat in silence, the car barely creeping forward inch by inch. Harper could feel Connor's irritation ratcheting up with every passing minute, every unmoving car in front of them. The lack of sleep, the hunger gnawing at both of them—it was a volatile mix, and she knew it wouldn't take much to push either of them over the edge.

She turned her attention to the side of the highway, catching a flicker of movement. A handful of cars had started veering off, bumping their way onto a dirt road that cut through the trees. Harper narrowed her eyes, watching them disappear into the shadows.

It wasn't on the GPS. But it was a way out.

Harper pointed out the line of cars leaving the highway. "Hey, look at those cars."

Connor barely looked up from the GPS. "I wonder where

that takes them," he muttered, zooming out on the map to trace the road's path. His fingers moved around, eyes scanning for a shortcut. "It cuts through town, but I'm not sure it would save us time," he admitted, irritation creeping into his voice.

Harper leaned over. "It's worth a try. If it cuts through the town, we can reach the highway on the other side and hopefully bypass the traffic here."

Connor rubbed his jaw as he weighed the risks. Harper could imagine what he was thinking—every second they sat in traffic ate into the schedule, but an unknown dirt road? That could be worse.

Harper saw his hesitation and pressed on. "C'mon, what's the worst that can happen? We can always turn around if we have to. Besides, at least those cars are going somewhere."

Connor let out a sharp breath. "Or they're blindly following each other." He tapped the steering wheel. "We should stick to the main road."

Harper shook her head. "Better to be moving than sitting here for hours."

Connor clenched his jaw and flicked on the blinker. "Fine. We'll try it."

He weaved through impatient drivers, merging toward the narrow turnoff. Gravel crunched under the tires as they left the highway behind, following the few cars that had chosen the same escape route. Harper felt a wave of relief as the gridlocked traffic shrank in the rearview. Even Connor seemed to exhale a little until the road worsened.

The asphalt gave way to uneven dirt, riddled with potholes and loose stones. The car jostled with each bump.

Harper snuck a glance over her shoulder. "That's weird. I thought more people would follow us."

Connor flexed his fingers. His clenched tight. "Knew this was a mistake," he muttered, voice edged with regret.

Then it happened.

A sharp, metallic pop split the air as the car jolted hard to the side. Connor's knuckles went white on the wheel, jaw locked as he wrestled it straight. Gravel spat from beneath the tires as they skidded, then thudded to a stop on the shoulder. Up ahead, the taillights of the last car vanished around a bend.

Harper's pulse roared in her ears. She stared at Connor—his brows drawn tight, lips pressed into a line, a muscle ticking in his cheek.

Fumbling with her seatbelt, she pushed the door open and stepped out. Heat and dust surged up around her ankles as she walked to the back of the car. The rear right tire sagged in ruin, its rubber flayed in strips, cords exposed like muscle.

Connor joined her, dragging a hand through his hair. "Jesus Christ. Of course."

Harper stared at the ruined tire. The guilt crept in faster than the panic, hot and suffocating. She wished she could rewind ten minutes. She'd pushed him into this. And now here they were, stranded on the side of the road with a shredded tire. Harper watched helplessly as Connor's expression shifted from frustration to anger.

"There's gotta be a donut in the trunk," she said, trying to sound more confident than she felt. "Do you... know how to change a tire?"

Connor shot her a look. "Of course I do."

She raised her hands. "Just asking. A lot of guys don't."

Connor's expression darkened. "Like Nate?"

Harper froze. A flicker of memory surfaced—she and Nate stranded on the shoulder of I-87, him clueless and yelling at her as she called her mom in tears. Harper's jaw tensed. "Don't expect any help from me," she muttered, dropping onto the dusty roadside with her arms crossed.

Connor shook his head and walked to the trunk. He hauled out the spare and the jack and set to work without saying a word.

Harper watched from her spot in the dirt, impressed. He moved with confidence, every motion deliberate. But when he hit a snag, fighting with a stuck lug nut, she rolled her eyes and pushed to her feet.

"Here," she said, kneeling beside him.

He blinked at her in surprise. "Thanks."

She didn't respond. They didn't speak as both were focused on the task, while the early summer sun blazed overhead, growing too hot for comfort. Dust clung to Harper's arms. Hunger curled in her gut, sharper now, and when her stomach growled, she prayed Connor didn't hear it.

No such luck. He glanced over. Harper looked away fast, heat blooming in her cheeks.

He tightened the last bolt and leaned away, wiping sweat from his forehead with the edge of his shirt. As he did, the fabric lifted just enough for Harper to catch a glimpse of his toned abs. Her eyes lingered a second too long before she jolted into awareness, quickly turning away and pretending to brush dirt off her jeans.

They climbed into the car again, and Harper had the AC blasting the moment the doors shut with a dull thud. Connor drove slower now, the donut spare forcing a cautious pace.

After a while, he muttered, "We're not getting to California on this thing. We'll need a real tire. Soon."

Harper gave a small, guilty smile. "I didn't think the road

would be that bad."

He gave a humorless snort. "Yeah, well. You can't always see what's coming."

She waited, expecting blame, but his tone wasn't sharp, only tired.

The pressure behind her eyes built until it broke—a slow overflow of exhaustion, stress, and everything they'd carried since the start of this trip. Harper blinked fast, trying to hold it in, but a single tear slipped free anyway. She wiped it away quickly, hoping Connor hadn't noticed.

He did.

He sighed and stared out the window before speaking. "Look. I was a dick earlier."

Harper eyed him as she quickly wiped away the tears. "What?"

"I shouldn't have brought up Nate," he said, eyes fixed on some distant point outside. "That was low. You didn't deserve it. None of this is your fault."

She didn't say anything for a beat, caught off guard by the apology, by how honest it sounded. The usual defensive reply didn't come. Instead, she simply said, "Thanks."

But something in her voice made him glance at her.

"I mean it," he added. "I've been... carrying my own shit, and sometimes it's easier to throw a punch than deal with it. Or say something I don't mean."

Harper swallowed hard. She wasn't sure what she was supposed to say to that.

But all she managed was, "Apology accepted."

It wasn't perfect, but it was enough for now.

Connor gave a short nod and shifted his gaze to the road ahead, the tension between them easing into something new. Not fixed. But different.

When a small town came into view, Harper leaned forward, squinting at the faded sign above the gas station.

"Thank God," she murmured.

Connor smirked. "You can say that again."

He spotted a tire shop off the main road. It was a squat, sun-faded building with rusted signage and a row of cars parked haphazardly out front. Connor pulled into the lot, gravel crunching beneath the tires, and exhaled, the tension easing from his shoulders. Harper felt it, too.

Inside, the receptionist, a tired-looking woman thumbing through a magazine, didn't even glance up as she muttered that it'd be at least an hour after Connor explained their problem. He gave a nod of thanks and looked around at Harper. He tilted his head toward the diner next door, and she gave him a grateful look. At least they were on the same page about getting some food.

As soon as they stepped inside the diner, the sharp chill of the air-conditioning hit them, carrying with it the mouthwatering scent of buttery toast, grilled onions, and something sweet like cinnamon pancakes or fresh pie warming behind the counter. It was a sharp contrast to the heat outside, and Harper paused, eyes closing for a split second as she took it in. Her stomach growled so loudly that it echoed slightly in the booth-lined space, and she couldn't help but laugh.

Connor gave her a sidelong look, one brow arched. The corner of his mouth tugged upward, his first real smile since the trip began. "Well," he said, voice low and amused, "I guess that means we're in the right spot."

Harper rolled her eyes, but the smile pulling at her lips was genuine. A waitress, her apron dotted with stains, motioned toward a nearby booth. They both collapsed into the vinyl seats, the weight of exhaustion lifting as the promise of a real meal began to settle in.

When the food arrived, they devoured it with desperate hunger.. Harper practically inhaled her burger, only pausing when her fingers grew slick with grease. Across from her, Connor was doing the same, hunched over his plate like someone might steal it.

By the time they finished, they leaned back in unison, sighing in satisfaction. Their eyes met, and they both burst out laughing.

The moment of lightness was shattered by Connor's phone buzzing on the table. He looked down, his brow furrowing. "It's the tire place. Maybe they're done."

Harper watched as he answered. Not even a minute into the conversation and his expression hardened, the flicker of hope fading from his eyes. "Wait, what? I don't have time to wait around." His voice dropped into a frustrated growl, his fingers running through his hair. Harper sat up straight, sensing something was wrong.

Connor exhaled sharply, muttering under his breath before speaking up. "I'm coming over." He ended the call and looked at her, the lines of his jaw tense with frustration. "The tire shop says the alignment's shot from driving on the donut over that rough road. They won't have it ready until tomorrow—if they can even get the parts in time." He shook his head, exasperation rolling off him in waves. "This is bullshit."

Harper saw the weight of it settle on him, and she swiftly spoke up. "Okay, I'll take care of the bill and meet you over there."

Connor didn't hesitate, nodding curtly as he grabbed his phone and stood. He walked out of the diner without another word, his posture rigid. Harper watched him go, bracing herself for the kind of mood that would follow their delay. With a weary glance, she flagged down the waitress to settle the bill before making her way to the tire shop.

When she stepped outside, Connor stood by the curb, arms crossed beside their suitcases and bags. His shoulders were stiff, his entire body coiled tight, a spring ready to snap. The moment he caught sight of her, he didn't hesitate. "I tried to get them to move faster," he said, his voice low and taut."But we're stuck here until tomorrow. Maybe we should start looking for another rental."

Harper looked at him for a beat before asking, "How bad are we on time?"

Connor exhaled, clearly reluctant to admit it. "We have about a two-day buffer, but I didn't want to push it and risk being late."

Harper folded her arms. "Would've been nice to know that before you were freaking out over every little thing and acting like a total tight ass about driving nonstop."

Connor opened his mouth to argue, but Harper held up a hand. "That being said, getting another rental wouldn't help now. We're both exhausted. We've barely slept. If we push through another ten, twelve hours on the road, we could end up in an accident."

She saw the gears turning in his head, so she pushed further. "We might as well use this time to get a hotel and sleep."

Connor paced for a second before relenting. "Yeah, I guess you're right. That makes more sense."

Harper threw up her hands. "Thank you."

Connor started to look through his phone. "We can probably Uber to a nearby hotel."

Harper scanned the area and spotted a large Hilton sign within walking distance. She pointed. "Look, there's one over there."

Connor followed her gaze and said, "Let's go."

They started walking, the route winding through the town's charming downtown area. Harper took in the mix of old and new: antique shops nestled between sleek coffee spots, and trendy restaurants tucked beside classic diners. It was the kind of place that effortlessly pulled in travelers.

She pointed to a bar with a string-lit patio. "Look! We should check this place out tonight."

Connor barely spared it a glance. "No. We'll stick to the hotel until the car's ready."

Harper rolled her eyes and playfully punched his arm. "Come on, if we're stuck here, we might as well have some fun."

Connor shook his head, unimpressed.

Harper shrugged, her tone clipped. "Fine. We don't have to stick together. You can sulk in the hotel, and I'll go check it out myself."

Connor stopped dead in his tracks. "You're not going alone."

She spun around to face him, one brow arched. "And why the hell not?"

He hesitated, jaw working, before saying, "We don't know this town. You don't know what kind of people go to that bar."

Harper let out a short, bitter laugh. "God, you worry too much."

Connor's eyes narrowed. "And you don't worry enough."

They stared each other down, words hanging heavy between them. The air crackled with tension—neither willing to yield, both too tired to keep arguing, yet too stubborn to let it drop. Without a word, they turned and resumed walking.

By the time they reached the hotel, the air had thickened between them.

Connor stepped up to the front desk without a word and pulled out his wallet. Harper didn't argue. Neither of them mentioned getting two rooms. This time, it felt pointless.

When they opened the door to their room, Harper let out a soft breath of relief. Two beds.

It wasn't much, dated furniture, and plain walls, but the cool air and the promise of clean sheets were the height of luxury after being in the dusty sun.

Harper walked toward the bed closest to the window when Connor's voice followed, light with amusement. "Well, at least I won't have to worry about you stealing the covers all night."

She shot him a look. "Yeah, and I don't have to worry about your giant body taking up the entire bed."

Connor chuckled as he dropped his bag. They went through the usual motions of plugging in their phones and kicking off their shoes. Fatigue crashed into Harper in a sudden wave. She glanced at Connor. "Mind if I close the curtains? I'm going to try to sleep."

He shook his head. "Go ahead. I'm close to passing out myself."

Exhaustion claimed Harper the moment she collapsed onto the bed. When she woke, it felt as if only minutes had passed. Her body was heavy with grogginess, the dim room spinning slightly around her. She reached for her phone: 5:30 p.m. A weary sigh escaped as she pushed herself up, rubbing her eyes in a slow, futile attempt to clear the fog. She looked to the other bed, where Connor was still asleep, one arm draped over his face. Harper's eyes were drawn once more to the scar on his arm, the story behind it still a mystery. She hadn't asked. Not yet.

Knowing sleep wouldn't come this time, she climbed out of bed and grabbed fresh clothes from her suitcase. After a long, hot shower, she felt human once more.

When she stepped out of the bathroom, Connor was awake, scrolling through his phone. He glanced up. "Hey. Just woke up."

"I woke up a little while ago," she said, toweling off her hair.

Connor shook his head. "Can't believe we slept for so many hours."

Harper chuckled. "It's been an exhausting trip so far."

"That's for sure." He hesitated before adding, "No weird knocks on the door?"

"Nope," she said. "So far, we're in the clear."

"Good." He looked as if he wanted to say more, but let it go. Instead, he grabbed his things and disappeared into the bathroom.

Harper gathered her hair into a loose bun and applied a light touch of makeup, grateful to see that her eyes lost some of the earlier fatigue and dullness. The mirror was kinder now, offering her a slight sense of renewal.

A few minutes later, Connor emerged from the bathroom in a simple pair of jeans and a t-shirt, his casual outfit mirroring hers. He paused, rubbing the back of his neck with an almost distracted air. "I've been thinking," he said.

Harper raised an eyebrow. "That's dangerous."

Connor ignored her jab, his eyes steady as he continued, "I think we should check out that bar you mentioned. Might be good to blow off some steam."

Harper's jaw dropped in mock shock. "Who are you, and what did you do with Connor?"

A small laugh escaped him, his lips curling slightly. "We're not staying out all night, but a quick dinner and a drink won't kill us. Plus, I'll probably be awake for hours after crashing all day."

Harper's face lit up with a wide grin. "Oh my God, I can't believe you said that! Give me a second to, you know, look a little less like I rolled out of bed."

"You don't have to do much," Connor said, his voice quieter now, almost shy. "You look great."

Harper froze for a brief moment, surprised by the unexpected compliment.

Connor seemed to realize what he'd said almost instantly. His eyes darted away as he fumbled for his phone, pretending it hadn't slipped out. Harper held in a small smile, the moment too fleeting to let herself dwell on.

She headed to the bathroom, finishing her makeup with a little extra focus on her eyes. They were her best feature, or so past compliments had always pointed out. Grateful she'd packed a sundress, she slipped into the light blue fabric, knowing how it made her eyes pop and how perfectly it hugged her curves.

When she stepped into the room, Connor was standing near the window, rolling up the sleeves of an olive green button-down that made his brown eyes look even darker. The shirt clung to his shoulders, and Harper caught herself admiring the muscles in his forearms as he finished with the last fold. He wore it with his usual jeans, somehow managing to make the casual look effortless.

She barely had time to school her expression before his gaze swept over her—and immediately darted away, like he hadn't meant to look.

Harper couldn't help but feel a flicker of warmth, but she pushed it aside. There was no point in reading into things with him.

So, shaking off the thoughts, she put her essentials in her small purse, and they headed out of the hotel together.

The warm evening air settled around them. A light buzz of excitement stirred in Harper's chest, a feeling she hadn't experienced in a while, not after everything that had happened. As they walked through the lively downtown, the sounds of music and laughter led them to the bar she'd spotted earlier. The light pop music spilled out onto the street, blending with the chatter of the crowd.

Connor opened the door for her, and as she stepped inside, an unmistakable sense of change lingered in the air. The tension from the start of the trip hung between them, heavy yet strangely lighter, as if the weight had found its balance. Perhaps they were beginning to understand each other in ways they hadn't before. Or maybe it was the long trip, playing tricks on their minds. Whatever it was, Harper couldn't help but feel that tonight might be the start of something different.

Seven

Day 2: Are You Kidding Me

❧

The bar had the kind of atmosphere that made it easy to forget about the world outside. There was dim lighting, the scent of fried food and beer hanging in the air, and a steady hum of chatter beneath the music. A hostess greeted them and led them to a high-top table off to the side. From here, Harper could take in the whole layout: pool tables, dartboards, and other bar games scattered around the space. It was bigger than it had seemed from the outside, the kind of place that invited you to stay for hours.

Harper leaned toward Connor, eyes alight. "We have to try everything."

Connor smirked. "Slow down, killer. Let's start with a drink first."

She grinned as the waitress appeared, and they ordered their drinks—a beer for him and a lemon drop for her, along with typical bar food.

By the time their food arrived, Harper was halfway through her drink, feeling lighter than she had in days. She popped a fry in her mouth and tilted her head toward Connor. "You know, I get the feeling that you might be more fun than I thought."

Connor smiled a bit, lifting his beer. "I can be a lot of fun." Harper raised a brow. "Maybe getting to know you wouldn't be so bad." Connor met her gaze, something unreadable flickering in his brown eyes. "Same."

The light caught the scar on Connor's cheek, and for a moment, Harper's attention lingered there. She hadn't asked about the marks on his skin, the one on his cheek, the one on his arm, but tonight, maybe she'd ask.

Connor's improved mood brought a sudden warmth, but before she could linger on it, another curiosity took hold. She rested her chin on her hand. "Okay, serious question. Are you single? Or is that Allison chick waiting for you in New York?"

A subtle change crossed Connor's face, enough for Harper to notice. He didn't look away, but something guarded settled in his posture. He paused mid-sip, clearly not expecting that. "I'm single."

Harper let out a breath she hadn't realized she'd been holding. She pushed a little further. "Okay, so who's Allison?"

His expression dimmed, hands pressing harder against the bottle."We dated for a bit over a year." He looked at her, noting the surprise on her face. "She wanted more, but I wasn't ready. So I ended it a few months ago."

Harper's eyes twinkled as she said, "Let me guess, she's the reason you hate country music?"

Connor let out a small chuckle. "You put that together, huh?"

She grinned. "I'm good at reading people."

Connor exhaled, raking a hand through his tousled hair.

"She's an aspiring country singer. When she decided to move to Nashville, she wanted me to come with her." His voice grew somber. "That's when I realized I couldn't give her what she wanted."

He stared at the table for a second before looking up. "Maybe not ever."

Harper studied him. "How do you feel about it now? If you can't even listen to country music, I imagine it still stings."

Connor took a slow sip of his beer before answering. "I think I'm more mad at myself for not feeling worse. I know I made the right choice. But hearing country music reminds me of all the time we wasted trying to fix something that was broken from the start."

Harper's voice was low, barely more than a breath. "It's not really over for her, is it?"

Connor turned to her, surprise flickering across his face.

"The texts," she added swiftly. "I wasn't trying to snoop or anything… but you have to agree that she was lighting up your phone."

A crooked smile tugged at his lips. "I can't be mad at you for noticing. Allison's been trying to patch things up. But… It's not going to happen."

Harper gave a nod, looking away, but not before relief washed over her features. She hadn't realized how much she wanted to hear that.

For a moment, neither of them spoke. They took slow sips of their drinks, the pause between words easy and unforced. Connor shifted the tone and steered the conversation. "Enough about me. You mentioned something about a new job in California?"

Harper felt relieved that he hadn't brought up Nate. She

nodded. "Yeah, for a lifestyle brand based over there. I'm hoping this leads to more opportunities down the line."

She wavered, debating how much to share. But when she met Connor's inquisitive look, she found herself continuing. "Nate always downplayed what I did. Made me feel small. I started believing there was something wrong with me because I wasn't chasing some flashy, high-stakes job the way he was." Harper paused for a second before adding, "He's a lawyer." Connor gave a knowing nod. She let out a breath. "This project gave me the confidence I needed to walk away. And I know life's going to be better away from all that toxicity."

Silence hung between them until Connor reached across the table, his fingers grazing hers in a warm, steady touch. "I know I said it earlier, but… you're brave for leaving," he said, his voice low and certain. "That takes a hell of a lot of courage."

He hesitated briefly before continuing, "I knew someone… a friend. She was in a similar situation. It took her ages to get out. I saw what it did to her and how much time it took for her to believe she deserved better."

Harper's throat tightened unexpectedly, the weight of his words settling in. "Thank you," she said softly, feeling something shift between them.

As if on cue, their moment was interrupted by the waitress coming to check on them. Harper flashed a small smile, grateful for the distraction, and ordered another round of drinks. She didn't mind. The air between her and Connor felt easier now.

The rest of the night unfolded with ease; it had a different energy, one that was lighter and more fun. They played darts, pool, and whatever random bar game they could find, laughing at their poor attempts and the awkward misfires. Harper found herself letting go in a way she hadn't realized she needed to, the constant weight of her past and the shadow of Nate's presence slowly fading from her mind.

There was a relief in that, a peace she hadn't expected to find here. The slimy guy who showed up at the motel didn't seem to be anywhere close to them now, and for the first time, the thought of Nate possibly following her wasn't on her mind. It was she and Connor, living in the moment.

And Connor, despite his usual broody demeanor, turned out to be the perfect partner-in-crime.

Several drinks later, the music swelled, and the small dance floor filled with people. Harper's eyes lit up. "C'mon, let's dance!"

Connor shook his head, his smile half-amused, half-resigned. "I don't dance."

Harper grinned and grabbed his hand. "Oh, come on. It's not rocket science."

To her surprise, he didn't resist. Instead, he let her pull him onto the dance floor as the speakers blasted a familiar pop song. They moved together effortlessly, Harper swaying to the beat as Connor's hands found her waist.

The heat of his touch was impossible to ignore, his body molding easily to hers as they danced. The beat of the song pulsed through the air, quick and carefree, and Harper swayed with it, laughing lightly as they moved together.

The music gradually slowed, the lively tempo fading into a softer, slower melody. Harper instinctively pulled away, but before she could put distance between them, Connor grabbed her wrist and pulled her closer to him.

Her heart skipped. She looked up at him, startled by the sudden closeness. His hand slid to the small of her back, pulling her in with urgency. His other hand grazed the nape of her neck, his fingers brushing over her skin in a way that made her breath catch.

The air between them seemed to hum with electricity. Connor's scent, whiskey, and something familiar wrapped around her, making her pulse race. As she tilted her head slightly, her eyes caught on the scar that curved faintly along his cheekbone, visible even in the dim lighting.

"Can I ask…" she murmured, her voice barely above the music. "What happened? Your scar."

Connor's eyes flicked away for the briefest second. The warmth in his eyes cooled slightly, not unkind, but guarded.

"Not tonight," he said softly. "Not yet."

Harper nodded, her fingers brushing lightly over the fabric of his button-down. She didn't press. Whatever that story was, it wasn't ready to be told.

Their bodies stayed close, swaying gently to the music, neither speaking. A peacefulness settled between them, not awkward, but charged. Harper's eyes glanced at Connor's lips before returning to meet his gaze. The moment hung heavy, suspended in silence.

Connor leaned in slowly this time, his movements careful and unhurried. Harper didn't back away. She closed the gap, tilting her chin to meet him halfway.

Harper's breath caught as Connor's lips brushed hers—tentative at first, as if he was giving her an out. But she didn't take it. Couldn't. Her fingers slid to the back of his neck, holding him there like maybe if she stayed close enough, this would all make sense.

She tasted the whiskey on his lips, and breathed in the mix of soap and something uniquely him. His lips moved with hers slowly, every touch heavy with meaning, awakening feelings she hadn't expected.

He wasn't rushing; he was memorizing. And with every careful, deliberate kiss, Harper could feel herself slipping, sinking into something she hadn't meant to want.

Connor's hand moved to her waist, grounding her, but there was something hesitant in the way he touched her. He pulled away slightly, and for a second their eyes met, his unreadable, hers wide and uncertain. For a moment, she thought he might say something, might change his mind.

So she kissed him again. Harder this time. Because she didn't want to think. Not yet.

And still, neither of them let go.

Then— "Hey!"

A sharp voice cut through the air, making Harper's heart skip.

Connor instantly recoiled, his hands moving to shield her, pushing her behind him as if instinctively protecting her from whatever was coming. The moment shattered as the energy between them shifted from playful to tense. Harper barely had time to process before she saw him.

Nate.

He stood there, a few feet away, a storm of anger contorting his face. His posture was stiff, his hands balled into fists at his sides. His eyes darted between Harper and Connor, but when they locked onto Connor, pure venom burned in them. The air crackled with aggression.

Harper opened her mouth to speak, to ask what was going on, but before she could even form the words, Nate moved.

He swung.

Nate's fist came from nowhere, a blur of motion, and it connected with Connor's jaw with a sickening crack. The sound rang out, loud and violent. Harper gasped, her blood running cold, the world spinning as she watched Connor stagger from the blow. The chaos around them erupted in a storm of shouting voices and scraping chairs.

Connor didn't flinch for long. Barely missing a beat, he surged forward, his body colliding with Nate's. The force of the hit sent them crashing into a nearby table, with glasses shattering and liquid splashing across the floor.

"Stop it! Stop!" Harper shouted, but her voice barely rose above the roar of the bar. She shoved through the cluster of onlookers with her eyes locked on the mayhem in the center of the room. The space buzzed with the noise of glass breaking, people shouting, and fists colliding with flesh.

Connor held his ground, steady and calculated, while Nate fought with the desperation of someone who had nothing left to lose. His swings were wild and unpredictable, each strike fueled by a deeper rage. A rage that was aimed to hurt more than just Connor, trying to shatter something that had been gnawing at him long before tonight.

Both men crashed into a table, sending bottles and half-filled glasses flying. One shattered near Harper's feet. She barely flinched.

She was right beside them now. She knew she couldn't stop the fight, but she had to try. Harper's arms shot out instinctively, a desperate attempt to shove them apart, to say something, *anything*, to make it stop.

But before the words could leave her mouth, Nate spun. He was off-balance from Connor's last hit, his elbow swinging wide and wild.

Crack.

A burst of white-hot pain exploded across Harper's temple. Her breath caught. Her knees gave out.

The world tilted sideways.

Harper hit the ground hard, the thud of her body lost in the frenzy. The floor was sticky with spilled beer, shards of glass pressing into her hands. Everything faded for a second—people's faces, the ceiling lights, even the sounds—before snapping into focus.

Her head throbbed. Her fingers came away wet when she touched the side of her face. Blood.

"Harper!" Connor's voice sliced through the madness.

She blinked up at him, dazed. He looked like a caged animal—face bloodied, fists clenched, chest heaving. His eyes were locked on her now, wild with panic, even as Nate tried to lunge at him once more.

The wail of sirens cut through the air.

Blue and red lights strobed through the front windows. The doors slammed open and several officers charged in, shouting commands that barely registered through the adrenaline haze.

One officer tackled Nate into a booth while another grabbed Connor's arms and wrenched them behind his back.

Blood trickled from Connor's split lip. Nate's one eye swelled shut as his face puffed up. Both of them breathed hard, like they'd just run a marathon.

Harper pushed herself up slowly, her skull pounding. She winced as she sat upright, wiping blood from her brow with a shaking hand. Her vision doubled for a second, but she forced herself to stay conscious and keep watching.

Connor looked at her as the cuffs clicked shut.

His eyes found hers. They were still a little wild, still catching up to what had happened. But even through the haze, she could see it: he was checking her over, not himself. Making sure she was okay.

Harper wanted to say something, but she couldn't move. Couldn't speak.

She sat there on the dirty bar floor, her face bleeding, heart pounding, and watched the officers drag Connor and Nate toward the door.

Harper forced her legs to move, stumbling slightly as she approached the nearest officer. Her mouth felt dry, and her voice sounded strange—almost as if it didn't belong to her. "Where are you taking them?" she managed to ask, the question hanging in the air, more of a plea than a demand for answers.

The officer looked her over as he responded, his words clipped, automatic. "Local station. They'll be processed there." But the name of the station barely registered. Her mind was elsewhere, too consumed with the image of Connor's face and the violence of the night that had unfolded in a matter of minutes.

One of the other officers paused, his eyes briefly flicking to her face. "You okay?" he asked, his voice surprisingly gentle.

Harper wiped her cheek instinctively and remembered the blood streaking her skin. She gave a quick, tight nod, trying to ignore the way her pulse was still racing. "I'm fine," she muttered, though she wasn't sure if she believed it herself. Without a word, the officer inclined his head and slipped out the door.

Harper stood frozen, her hands shaking at her sides.

She wanted to chase after them, to shout, to unravel the mess before it hardened into something permanent. Her heart pounded, wild and urgent, but her legs wouldn't move; they were frozen while her mind screamed for her to do something. Anything. Instead, she stood rooted, watching Connor vanish into the night, a silent witness to the fallout she couldn't stop, couldn't fix.

Eight

Day 2: Jail

Being buzzed didn't make it any easier for Harper to figure out how to get to the police station. One of the waitresses, who had been watching her closely ever since the fight broke out, approached with a concerned look as she noticed the blood on Harper's face.

"Hey, are you okay? You're bleeding."

Harper shrugged it off. "It's nothing, only a scratch. I'll be fine." Her words rang hollow as a headache pressed at her temples, sharp and insistent, but she pushed it down. She was lost somewhere in the mess of her thoughts, still trapped in the memory of Connor's face and the fight.

The waitress studied her for a beat, sensing Harper's distracted state. "The station's a bit far of a walk, but if you need a ride, I can help you get an Uber or call a cab," she suggested, her voice kind, offering practical help amid Harper's daze.

Harper nodded, grateful but too numb to fully process the

offer. "I can grab an Uber. Thanks, though."

Once the waitress stepped away to deal with the mess left behind, Harper slipped into the restroom.

Her hands were still trembling as she pulled out her phone and booked an Uber. She splashed cold water on her face, scrubbing at the blood with quick, impatient swipes. Her reflection stared up at her—drawn and disoriented. Harper exhaled slowly, grounding herself as best she could before pushing the door open and stepping once more into the dim, humming noise of the bar.

The place was still scattered with overturned chairs and broken glass, a few people lingering to watch the aftermath. Harper started toward the aftermath of the fight, instinctively offering to help, but the waitress from earlier shook her head.

"We've got it," the waitress said gently, giving Harper a look that was equal parts sympathy and knowing. "You should wait outside for your Uber. Your boyfriend needs you."

Harper didn't bother correcting her. The word *boyfriend* echoed inside her, a sharp reminder of the moment she and Connor had shared before everything went wrong. It stung more than she wanted to admit.

Without saying anything, she inclined her head and stepped out.

Harper went and sat on the curb, hugging her knees, staring at the dark sky and people walking down the street without a care in the world. Everything she'd been running from was catching up. And maybe she was a little scared it wasn't only Nate anymore.

Minutes later, the Uber pulled up, and Harper climbed in, her nerves on edge as the car carried her toward the police station.

Harper stepped out into the cool night; her whole body was

wrought with a strange mix of exhaustion and adrenaline as she the building in front of her pulsed with life. Several officers weaved through the entryway, voices cutting through the noise, a bitter smell hanging in the air.

It was clear that tonight was busier than most.

Once Harper stepped inside, the line at the front desk stretched long, inching forward under the gaze of a bored officer who looked exhausted from hours on the job. Time dragged on, each slow step making Harper more restless, more on edge. She wanted to move faster, to find Connor and get him out of here, but the line crept forward like molasses. Her thoughts kept drifting to him, and the weight of guilt for dragging him into her mess with Nate.

The noise in the station grew muffled around her as she waited, her fingers tapping nervously at her side. Her mind raced. Was Connor okay? What were they going to do to him? Was she too late? She hated this feeling of being small and powerless. She wanted to do something, anything, to fix it all. Harper checked the time on her phone and saw that it was after midnight.

When she finally reached the desk, the officer didn't even glance up at first, flipping through paperwork with the dull focus of someone halfway through a tiring shift. "Name?" he asked, his voice as flat and uninterested as the flickering fluorescent lights overhead.

"Connor Hale," Harper said.

That made him look up. His eyes narrowed slightly, recognition flickering across his face. "The one from the bar fight?"

Harper flinched at the mention, the image of fists and blood flashing behind her eyes. She nodded.

With a tired shake of his head, the officer turned to his forms.

"Both of them are being booked. You'll have to wait until a judge sets bail. Could be a while."

His tone made it sound as if she were asking about a parking ticket, not someone she cared about. Harper opened her mouth to say something, but she wasn't even sure what, and nothing came out. The officer had moved on to the person behind her.

With nowhere else to go, Harper dropped into one of the hard plastic chairs in the waiting room. Adrenaline that had carried her this far was fading fast, replaced by a dull, bone-deep exhaustion. Above her, fluorescent lights hummed, their flicker echoing her fatigue.

She folded her arms around her middle, trying to get comfortable in the rigid chair. A dull throb pulsed at the side of her head where Nate's elbow had caught her, but she ignored it. At some point, sleep crept in without warning. Her head leaned against the wall, her breath slow and shallow.

Harper didn't know how long she'd been out until a hand gently shook her shoulder.

She startled awake, heart thudding as she blinked into the harsh light. Everything felt a little sideways, the leftover alcohol in her system making the room swim slightly.

"You here for Connor Hale?" a uniformed officer asked, his tone surprisingly soft.

Harper blinked up at him, still foggy. "Yeah," she said, voice hoarse.

The officer held up a clipboard. "Judge set bail. Four hundred dollars if you want to get him out tonight."

"Yes," Harper said hastily, the word tumbling out as she sat up straighter. "I'll pay it."

She gathered her things with clumsy hands, her balance still slightly off as she followed the officer down a corridor. Her heart thudded with each step, the hallway stretching endlessly in front of her. After the paperwork was squared away and the payment processed, the officer gestured for her to follow.

"This way."

They headed toward the holding area, a dim space that smelled of old coffee and disinfectant. Harper stepped inside and froze. She locked on Connor first, shifting quickly to Nate.

Connor and Nate stood on opposite sides of the cell, both bruised and bloodied. Connor's shirt was torn, and there was dried blood at the corner of his mouth. Nate looked worse; his eye was swollen, his nose seemed slightly bent, and his jaw was tight with tension. Neither of them was speaking, their glares fixed on opposite walls.

As Harper stepped closer, both men turned as if they'd sensed her before she appeared.

Connor's stance eased first and there was a flicker of relief crossed his face, subtle enough to miss, but Harper caught it. His eyes met hers, and for a brief moment, he seemed to finally relax.

"Connor," she breathed, rushing forward. Her voice broke halfway through his name. "Are you okay?"

He stepped closer to her on the opposite side of the bars, slowly, with a wince that sent a fresh wave of guilt crashing over her. Still, he managed a crooked half-smile. "I am now."

The officer beside the cell didn't say anything at first. He slid the key into the lock and twisted it. The clunk of the latch falling away echoed too loudly throughout the room, and the door creaked open.

"She posted your bail," the officer said to Connor without ceremony. "You're free to go."

Connor's face snapped to her, stunned. "You didn't have to

do that."

"I know," Harper said softly. Her voice barely carried. "But I wanted to."

There was a moment where neither of them moved. Something flickered in Connor's expression like he wanted to say more, but couldn't quite find the words.

Then Nate stepped forward.

"Harper." His voice was different from what she expected. Rough. Almost pleading.

She turned to him, her face hardening in an instant. "What the hell are you doing here?" The warmth in her voice was gone, as if it had been carved out and discarded. "How did you even find me?"

Connor stepped out of the open cell, moving to stand beside her without a word.

Nate hesitated. "I..."

The officer cut in, voice sharp, slicing through the tension. "If I were you, I'd go with the truth. We ran your record."

Connor shot Harper a look, and she braced herself.

The officer crossed his arms. "Multiple outstanding warrants for assault. That's why he's not going anywhere."

Harper stared at the officer, stunned. Her eyes locked on Nate. "Assault? Seriously?"

He shifted, jaw tight. "It's not what you think."

"Then tell me what it is," she snapped. "Because you have about ten seconds to explain how the hell you even found me."

Nate's gaze faltered. "I've been tracking your phone."

The words struck her. Harper flinched, air stolen from her lungs, fury rising in a slow, searing wave. "You've been what?"

His voice dipped, grasping at calm. "Started a couple of months before we broke up. I... I just wanted to make sure you were safe."

She stared at him as if seeing a stranger. "No. You wanted control." Her hands shook.

"It wasn't—"

"It was," she cut in, voice unsteady but sharp. She turned to the officer. "Does he have his phone? I want to watch him shut off the tracking. Now."

The officer gave a short nod, then reached behind the desk. "We pulled it when he came in."

He walked back over and held it out. Nate took it with a twitch of his hand, almost fumbling it.

Harper stepped closer, gaze locked and unflinching. "Do it."

Nate opened his settings, thumb moving with agonizing slowness. He turned off the location sharing. After a long, silent beat, he opened another app, something buried and unfamiliar. Connor leaned closer, watching his every move.

"There's another one," Nate muttered. "It's… not legal. I used it for work, but…" He didn't finish.

Harper's jaw clenched. "Delete it."

He did.

She turned to the officer, barely holding herself together. "What can I do to make sure this doesn't happen anymore?"

"Call your provider. Change your passwords. A full factory reset might help. And check your account access; he could've added a backup line without your permission."

With a quiet breath, Harper said, "Okay."

The officer retrieved Nate's phone and tucked it away in the desk. "He won't have access to this until late tomorrow. You have time."

Harper turned, ready to leave, but Nate's voice chased her to the door.

"You're making a mistake, Harper. You're gonna regret walking away from me."

She didn't slow. Didn't flinch. Her voice was steady, flat. "Go to hell."

The silence that followed hit harder than a shout. Even the officer shifted behind the desk, gaze flicking between them.

Harper didn't even realize she and Connor had walked through the station and out until the cool, early-morning air hit her.

Outside, the world felt hushed, with only the faintest hint of dawn bleeding across the horizon. Harper looked down at her phone: 4:02 a.m.

Their footsteps clicked against the sidewalk, each one ringing a little louder in the quiet. The sharpness of the night had faded, replaced by a heavy fatigue that settled deep in her bones. Harper's feet ached, her head throbbed in the background, no longer masked by the buzz of alcohol.

She glanced sideways. Connor's knuckles were raw, his shirt torn, a smear of dried blood near his lip.

Harper's voice came low. "I'm sorry you got dragged into my mess. Again."

He shrugged, but there was tension in his jaw. "Don't be. I've wanted to hit that guy since he cornered you at the diner."

Harper let out a surprised laugh, the sound lighter than she expected. "Same, actually. I'm a little jealous you beat me to it."

He glanced at her, something softer flickering across his bruised features. "Yeah, well…" His fingers lightly grazed her arm as they walked, a barely-there touch that made Harper's skin prickle. "I wouldn't want you getting hurt."

Connor stopped, turning to face her fully. His hand rose gently to her cheek, brushing beneath the spot where dried blood had once been and now where a light bruise was forming. "But you did."

Harper tensed, instinctively brushing his hand away. "It's nothing," she said, voice quick.

But Connor didn't move, didn't let it go as easily. His eyes stayed fixed on her, unreadable but intense. "I shouldn't have let Nate get that close to you."

Harper's heart pounded in her ribs. She looked up at him, really looked, taking in the bruise darkening his cheekbone, the small split on his lip, the way he seemed to be holding himself together through sheer will.

And for a second, she felt it again; his mouth on hers, the heat, the ache, before the night had shattered.

She didn't know if the memory crossed his mind too, but his expression changed. But instead of saying more, he let out a breath and turned toward the hotel.

"What a night," he muttered.

Harper let out a shaky breath. She dragged a hand through her hair, wincing as her fingers caught on a tangle. "No kidding," she muttered, her voice thin with fatigue.

Once they were in the hotel room, everything felt still. Too still.

Harper sank onto the edge of the bed, the adrenaline that had carried her this far bleeding out fast, leaving a hollow ache behind. Without thinking, she pulled out her phone. Her fingers moved on autopilot, dialing her provider, navigating menus, and answering security questions with a calm that didn't match the chaos still ringing in her bones.

She blocked Nate's number and changed her account password. Harper added every layer of protection the phone company offered. It didn't matter that her hands were shaking from pure exhaustion. She wasn't going to let Nate have any more control over her life.

While she handled everything on her phone, she stayed aware of Connor's every movement.

He didn't sit. Didn't speak. Just moved—shoes kicked off, charger plugged in, cleaned up in the bathroom, and began pacing without purpose.

His fingers twitched at his sides, restless.

Eventually, Connor stopped at the window, staring out at the empty lot. One hand hovered over the bruise on his cheek; the other curled into a loose fist he didn't seem to notice.

When she finished up, Harper let her phone fall to the bed with a soft thud. The weight of it, of everything, pressed into her all at once.

She cut her eyes towards the bathroom door, briefly considering the idea of a shower. But the thought of standing under too-bright lights, of peeling off her clothes and being alone with herself was too much. She was too tired. Too frayed.

So Harper stood and moved slowly to turn down the covers. Every step tugged at her limbs. Her heart thudded in her chest, heavy and uneven. She crawled into bed, each motion slower than the last.

From across the room, Connor moved to his bed and sat on the edge, his elbows braced on his knees as he faced away from her. He switched off the lamp between them, casting the room into soft shadow. "Goodnight," he murmured. His voice was low, slightly hoarse.

Harper stared at the ceiling. "Night," she whispered, unsure if he even heard it.

The calmness that followed was different than before. It wasn't empty. It was thick with everything they hadn't said.

The kiss. The fight. The look in Connor's eyes when he saw her at the station.

And worse, her questions. Was it real? Was it the drinks? Was it something that only made sense in the darkness and would vanish when they woke up?

Harper tugged the blanket tighter around her. She stayed that way for a long time, unmoving with her eyes wide open, listening to the rhythm of her breathing in sync with Connor's across the space between them.

Eventually, the ache in her body outweighed the heaviness inside her. Her eyes slipped shut, thoughts fading at the edges as sleep claimed her after one of the most exhausting nights she could remember.

Nine

Day 3: Change

Harper woke to a dull ache behind her eyes and the thick haze of a half-remembered nightmare pressing in. For a moment, she wondered if she'd imagined it all. The memories surfaced, sharp and sour. But one detail stood out with startling clarity: Connor's lips on hers.

She smiled at the thought, her fingers brushing absently over her mouth. But the warmth of the memory evaporated in an instant as the rest of the night flooded her mind. Nate. His sudden appearance, the fight, the arrest. The gut-wrenching realization that he'd been following her every step from the start. She exhaled slowly. At least that chapter of her life was over.

Rolling over, she eyed Connor's bed. He was still asleep, his face relaxed in a way she'd only seen glimpses of; for all his sharp edges and guarded stares, he looked almost peaceful. A version of him she felt she was only beginning to see.

Harper grabbed her phone from the nightstand: 11:33 a.m. She couldn't remember the last time she'd slept this late, but after the night they'd had, she was grateful for it. Careful not to wake Connor, she gathered some clothes and tiptoed to the bathroom.

She let the hot water scald her skin, hoping it could rinse away the knots in her shoulders. Process. Overthink. Repeat. What if the kiss had been a drunken mistake? What if it had meant something? She shut her eyes. Did she even want to know?

When she emerged, towel-drying her hair, she saw Connor stirring. He stretched, groaning slightly, before blinking at her.

"Morning," he mumbled, voice thick with sleep.

Harper hesitated for half a second before returning the greeting. "Morning."

There was an awkward pause as Harper went to sit on her bed and looked at Connor.

He ran a hand through his hair and asked, "What time is it?"

"Close to noon."

Connor sat up fast, grabbing his phone off the nightstand. "The tire place might have called."

He frowned at the screen—nothing—then let out a breath as he flopped back onto the bed.

The silence pressed in, thick and restless. Harper felt it creep under her skin until she couldn't sit with it anymore.

"How are you feeling?" she asked.

Connor turned his head slowly. His eyes were still glassy with sleep, lashes casting faint shadows below. He lifted a hand, fingertips grazing the split on his lip and his bruised cheek.

"Not the worst hangover," he said after a moment. "But my head's killing me."

She nodded. "Same."

Another pause.

Harper put the towel down and twisted it between her fingers, heart thudding. "How much do you remember?"

Connor's brow knitted in thought. "Well… the fight. Getting hauled to the station."

"Did we…?" He paused, wincing. "Was there a kiss?"

A flicker of something, almost apologetic, crossed his face.

Harper froze. That was it?

The moment that had looped in her head all night—the way he'd touched her, looked at her—meant so little that he had to ask?

Her stomach pitched. For a second, the room tilted. She stared at Connor, the blood roaring in her ears.

"You don't remember it?" she asked, her voice catching on the way out.

Connor dragged a hand through his hair, eyes distant. "It's all kind of a daze." He saw the way her face tightened, and an instant look of regret flitted across his face.

Harper's fingers tightened. "Right. Of course it is."

His eyes narrowed slightly, confused. "What's wrong?"

For a moment, she almost said nothing. But something in her cracked. She let out a short, humorless laugh. "What's wrong? Are you serious?"

He blinked, clearly not expecting the edge in her voice. "Yeah… I am."

She shook her head, turning away. The weight of disappointment settled deep within her ribs.

She remembered everything. The way he had pulled her in. The way his eyes softened when he looked at her. And now, he was looking at her as if none of it had ever happened.

"Forget it." She turned away, pretending to be busy by shoving clothes into her suitcase. She felt like an idiot.

Connor sat up, watching her. "Harper—"

"No. It's fine," Harper cut in, voice sharp, brittle. "Clearly, we were both drunk, and I was… a convenience."

Connor's expression twisted. "That's not—"

"Don't." She said as she turned to look at him with a mix of anger and hurt in her eyes. "I should've known better."

Connor pushed off the bed with a wince, dragging a hand over his jaw like he was trying to buy time. "That's not what this is. I didn't mean it like that. We were drinking. It just happened."

Harper's laugh was brittle, empty. It dropped into the quiet like a coin into a well. "Yeah. No shit."

Something shifted in his expression. Guilt. Regret. Anger. She couldn't tell.

"I told you how it was from the beginning," he said, voice flat now. "This wasn't supposed to mean anything. It's a ride, Harper. That's it."

She flinched, holding her breath a beat too long before looking away.

Her head throbbed, but she refused to let him retreat behind that cold, indifferent wall of his this time.

"You know what I think?" she snapped, stepping toward him. "I think you're terrified of letting anyone actually see you. So you play it safe. You pretend nothing matters."

Connor's eyes narrowed. "Oh, because you know me so well?"

"Say it," she said, now inches from him. "Say you're not attracted to me. Look me in the eye and say it, and I'll drop it."

He started to turn away, but she stepped in his path.

"Say it."

He exhaled hard through his nose, pacing two steps before spinning around. His voice was rough now, raw.

"Fine. You want honesty? Of course, I find you attractive. You drive me insane, but yeah. I notice you."

Her heart jumped. "Oh, I drive *you* insane?"

"Yes!" His voice rose. "Yes! With your smart-ass comments, your impulsive decisions—your way of always… always getting under my skin. And it's been, what? Two days? Two days, and I'm already losing my goddamn mind."

She took another step, close enough now to feel the heat radiating off his body.

"Maybe I wouldn't get under your skin if you gave a shit once in a while," she said, her breath catching.

They stood there, toe to toe, chest to chest, fury. The air between them crackled, hot and heavy. Harper could hear her pulse in her ears.

Connor's jaw was clenched, his fists at his sides. Harper's pulse pounded in her throat. For one heartbeat, the room seemed ready to collapse inward.

And then—

His phone buzzed.

The sharp sound sliced through the silence, shattering the moment.

Harper swallowed hard, stepping away as he gave her a hard look before grabbing his phone. He barely glanced at her as he answered.

"Yeah?" His expression shifted from annoyed to relieved. "Be there soon." He ended the call and looked over at Harper. "Car'll be ready in an hour."

She gave a curt nod and went back to gathering her things. Connor took a step closer. "Harper—"

Harper looked at him and held up a hand, stopping him mid-sentence. "Forget it, Connor. You're right. I'm reading too much into this." Her voice was calm, but there was a finality to it. She turned away, and he stood there, lips parted as if he wanted to say something, but nothing came.

They packed up, and after Connor took a quick shower, they left the hotel, the unspoken tension lingering between them. With time to kill before picking up the car, they headed to the same diner near the tire shop. As they reached the entrance, he held the door open. That gesture didn't change a goddamn thing. Harper refused to let it soften her. She wasn't the kind of girl to pine for attention from a man who clearly wasn't ready to give it.

They set their suitcases and bags down as they slid into the same booth as the day before, eating quietly, both avoiding eye contact. Harper stabbed at her food, trying to ignore the gnawing irritation burning inside her. Without warning, a piercing scream tore through the restaurant.

Every head snapped toward the source. A waitress burst out of the kitchen, panic written all over her face. "Is there a doctor here? Please, we need help!"

Harper's eyes widened as Connor slipped out of his seat, heading toward the woman. "I'm a doctor. What's going on?"

What? Harper blinked, stunned. Curiosity and concern propelled her to her feet, and she followed him toward the kitchen.

The waitress wrung her hands. "It's Frank—our manager. He collapsed in the kitchen. He's not moving, and he's not responding."

Connor pushed through the swinging doors with Harper at his heels. "When did it happen?"

"Just now. A minute ago—maybe less."

The kitchen was frozen in alarm. The sizzling of the grill and clatter of pans had stopped. Frank, a heavyset man in his sixties, was sprawled on the floor, motionless. Two line cooks hovered beside him, one trying to shake his shoulder, the other one looking on with his hand frozen over the phone.

"He just dropped," one of them stammered. "He said he felt lightheaded, next thing—boom. Hit the floor."

Connor knelt, two fingers at Frank's neck. His face went still in a professional, controlled way Harper hadn't seen before. His expression darkened. "It's faint."

He opened Frank's airway, angled his head, then interlocked his hands and began chest compressions with a quick, practiced rhythm. "You—" he pointed to one of the cooks, "—call 911. Say adult male, no pulse, possible sudden cardiac arrest. Tell them CPR's in progress."

The cook scrambled to obey, voice shaking as he relayed the information.

Harper stood frozen for a beat, watching this version of Connor. He was utterly focused, calm under pressure, and no hesitation in his movements.

Connor's hands pressed firmly and quickly on Frank's chest, his breaths counting the rhythm.

"Can I help?" Harper asked, voice tight.

"Yeah." He didn't pause. "Grab a folded towel, apron—anything soft. If he comes to, he might seize."

She snatched an apron from the counter, folded it fast, and knelt beside him.

"Good," Connor said. "If his airway clears, we roll him on his side. You support the head."

Sweat beaded on his forehead. The kitchen held its breath

with him.

Then—

A cough. Wet and jagged. Frank's body jerked under Connor's hands.

Connor instantly stopped compressions and turned him onto his side, stabilizing his head on Harper's makeshift cushion.

"He's breathing," he confirmed. "Shallow, but he's back."

A ripple of relief spread through the room just as sirens began to wail outside.

The paramedics burst in, and Connor stepped away to give them space, rubbing a hand over his face. He looked—not shaken, exactly. But his eyes had darkened, and the tension in his jaw wasn't stubbornness anymore.

Harper stood next to him as the EMTs took over, stabilizing Frank and preparing him for transport.

"You okay?" she asked softly.

Connor's eyes flicked to hers. "Yeah. Haven't done that in a while."

She studied him. "You were… kind of incredible, you know."

Connor's jaw flexed, uncertain how to handle the words. He stared at the kitchen floor, as if still lost in where his mind had been. After a beat, he let out a soft sigh. "We should get going. The car's probably ready by now."

They headed toward the front to settle their bill and grab their suitcases, but before they could reach the counter, the diner manager stopped them. "Hey, thank you. Seriously. You saved his life. Don't worry about paying for lunch." A few waitresses chimed in, voices overlapping with words—*hero, incredible*—floating through the air.

Harper watched Connor shrink beneath their praise, a man who could save a life without blinking but stiffened at compliments. "I'm glad he's okay," he said simply, voice low. Turning to Harper, "You ready?"

A quick dip of her chin said enough.

They stepped outside with their luggage, and a wall of heat hit them instantly. The early afternoon sun beat down from a washed-out sky. Harper fixed the strap of her backpack as they fell into step side by side, heading toward the tire shop down the block.

The streets were relatively silent, save for the occasional car passing by.

Harper kicked a stray pebble along the sidewalk, her voice pointed. "You said you were in the medical field when we first left New York, but you never actually told me what you did."

Connor let out a low exhale. "Didn't think it mattered."

She stopped walking, frowning as she turned to face him. "Didn't think it mattered? Connor, that's—" She broke off, running a hand through her hair, frustration sparking beneath the surface. "That's not nothing. You let me sit there thinking maybe you worked in a lab or handed out clipboards."

He met her eyes, steady but unreadable. "I wasn't trying to lie. I don't like how people react when I tell them I'm a doctor."

Harper shook her head, her voice softer now. "Maybe if you didn't keep hiding parts of yourself, you wouldn't have to worry about how people see you."

They stood there for a moment, neither of them looking away, until Harper began walking, her steps slower this time, the air between them heavier than before. She couldn't shake the sinking feeling in her chest, the sting of realizing she hadn't grown as close to Connor as she thought. All this time, all the miles they'd covered, and somehow he was still a stranger in all the ways that mattered.

The tire shop came into view, squat and sun-faded over the heat-shimmering pavement. Harper and Connor crossed the lot with their suitcases rolling noisily behind them. Inside, the sharp sting of burnt rubber and motor oil slammed into them. Fluorescent lights buzzed quietly overhead, casting a harsh, sterile glow over the grease-streaked counter and towering stacks of tires that loomed along the walls.

A mechanic behind the counter looked up, grease streaked across his hands and forearms. He sized them up. "You here for the grey sedan?"

Connor nodded. "That's us."

"She's ready to roll," the mechanic said, grabbing a clipboard from beneath the counter. "New tire, rebalanced everything, checked alignment while I was at it. $400 even."

Connor didn't hesitate. He shifted his bag, pulled out his wallet, and handed over his credit card. "Thanks."

The mechanic handed over the keys. "Safe travels."

Connor gave a nod and turned toward Harper, who was making her way to the exit. The sun pressed down on them as they stepped outside, heat radiating off the pavement. As they neared the car, Harper spoke.

"What's your Venmo?" she asked, pulling out her phone and opening the app. "I'll send you my half."

Connor shook his head. "Don't worry about it. Consider it payback for bailing me out."

Harper felt a flush creep up her neck at the reminder. She hated how easily she remembered why she'd had to bail him out, and worse, the way she still felt that damn kiss. Shaking off the thought, she shrugged. "Fine, guess that makes us square."

Connor gave a single nod, clearly in no hurry to revisit that night.

They reached the car and tucked their bags into the trunk, the thud of it closing echoing in the warm, open air. As they rounded the car at the same time, stopping short of the driver's door, their shoulders nearly brushed. A charged, wordless standoff.

Harper arched a brow. "You've driven most of the way. My turn."

Connor let out a breath. "Alright. But if you get tired, say something. We'll switch."

"Deal."

She slid into the driver's seat, moving it automatically, and he settled into the passenger side. It felt oddly natural, as if they'd done it a hundred times before.

The dashboard clock read a little after 1 p.m. They had to make good time today.

Connor plugged in the address for California, zooming in and out of the route, his brow furrowed. The GPS had them going across Oklahoma, and that stretch alone would take hours.

"Let's try to make it to Texas by tonight," Connor said, his voice clipped. "I don't want to make any unnecessary stops."

Harper offered a brief look before continuing from the tire shop to the highway ahead. The steady rhythm of tires on pavement rose to fill the noise between them, a subtle but persistent backdrop to everything left unsaid. Beside her, Connor sat with his arms crossed, eyes fixed on the stretch of pavement ahead.

She squeezed the wheel harder.

The burden of the last twenty-four hours settled deep inside her. This whole mess was her fault. She was the one who'd suggested the detour, the one who hadn't thought twice about taking the rough side road. If she hadn't, the tire wouldn't have blown. They wouldn't have had to get the car fixed. There would've been no small-town bar, no spiraling night, no Nate.

She shuddered at the thought of how close Nate had gotten. How easy it had been for him to find her.

But there was relief too. He was gone now. Out of her life, for real this time. And yet, guilt lingered under the surface.

Connor's dad's funeral was only days away. They had a buffer, sure, but not a big one. And every delay they'd had so far was because of her. The idea of them being late, of her being the reason he didn't make it on time, made her feel awful.

She cast a sidelong glance at Connor. He hadn't said much since they left the diner—maybe from exhaustion, or maybe because he was done with her.

Either way, she wasn't going to argue about stops. She'd already caused enough delays.

Once they hit cruising speed, Harper flipped through the radio until she landed on a station playing a mix of current hits and throwbacks. The GPS showed seventy miles of straight road ahead. Curiosity pulled her focus to Connor.

"So..." she started, her voice light but edged with something sharper as she looked down the road. "Are we not going to talk about the whole *surprise, I'm a doctor* thing?"

Connor's gaze landed on her, impossible to decipher. "I told you, I didn't think it was important."

She let out a soft scoff. "Not important? Kind of feels like a big detail to leave out. It would have been nice to know that from the beginning of this trip."

He raised a brow. "Was I supposed to tell you before or after your emergency gas station pit stop kicked off this whole trip?"

She shot him a look. "Sorry we can't all be superhumans. Some of us need snacks and functioning bladders before a cross-country drive."

Connor chuckled, the tension between them easing a little.

"But seriously," she said, "what kind of doctor are you?"

He hesitated, enough for her to notice, before replying, "Used to be a surgeon. Now I do primary care."

Harper studied him for a beat. Something about the way he said *used to be* piqued her interest. Before she could ask, he looked out the window, as if he'd already said too much.

"That's a pretty big shift," she said gently. "What made you change?"

Connor's jaw flexed. He stayed so quiet that she began to think he wouldn't answer. Finally, he said, "I was a neurosurgeon." He paused. "A good one." Another pause. "But I missed something on a routine case. The patient didn't make it."

The words hung there, heavy and low.

Harper's hands clenched the wheel. "I'm so sorry."

He looked down briefly before speaking. "The hospital cleared me, but I couldn't go back. I couldn't trust myself in the OR."

Harper's hand moved before she could stop it, fingers brushing his forearm. He covered her hand for a moment with a gentle but sure grip before letting go.

"I left New York for a while," he said. "When I returned, I wanted something more low-key. More stable. Somewhere I wasn't holding someone's life in my hands."

Harper gave a small smile. "So that's why you're such a control freak."

Connor let out a low laugh. "Yeah. I like knowing what's coming. I don't do well with uncertainty."

"You know that's life, right?" she said, glancing at him. "Uncertainty's kind of the whole deal."

He shrugged. "I don't have to control *everything*. Only the parts I can't risk messing up anymore."

"Like not making it to your dad's funeral?"

His eyes flicked to hers, surprised. "Exactly."

There was a pause.

"Is that what caused the rift between you two?" she asked.

He hesitated before giving a nod. "Yeah. You remember that?"

"I remember more than you think."

Connor gave a small, bitter smile. "He'd brag. My son, the brain surgeon. It meant something to him. Until it didn't, and when it all fell apart, I think he saw me differently. Or maybe I saw him differently."

"That's rough," Harper said. "Parents shouldn't only love the perfect versions of us."

"I looked up to him," Connor said. "He was… everything, for a long time. But after that, I stopped expecting him, or anyone, to be in my corner."

"So why go through all this to say goodbye?"

He looked straight ahead, his voice calm as he said, "Because he was still my dad. And for most of my life, he *was* in my corner. I'm there to say goodbye to *that* version of him."

Harper's voice was thick with emotion. "I hope you know… if we don't make it in time, that doesn't erase anything. You're still a good son. And a good person."

He flicked his eyes to her, a shadow crossing his face. "You still don't really know me."

Harper smiled softly. "Maybe not. But I know messed up when I see it. And I also know it doesn't cancel out the good."

Connor let out a breath that was a half-laugh, half-sigh. "Fair enough."

A while later, they pulled into a gas station off the highway.

The place looked half-abandoned, a flickering, sun-faded sign hanging crooked above the pumps. The afternoon heat clung to the air, heavy and unmoving.

Harper stretched as she climbed out, the stiffness of the drive settling in her bones. While she filled the tank, Connor disappeared inside.

When he returned, he wordlessly handed her a cold bottle of water. Their fingers brushed. Static snapped in her chest. She looked up. So did he. Neither of them said a word.

"I'll drive a bit more," Harper said, breaking the moment as she took a sip, her eyes fixed on the endless stretch of the horizon. "You can take over when it gets dark."

Connor inclined his head. "Deal."

Neither of them said anything else as they settled into their seats. Harper steered them onto the open road, the sun staying high in the sky behind them.

Hours later, the sky shifted from bruised purple to inky black, thick with electricity. It made Harper sit up straighter. It wasn't the slow fade of twilight; it was sudden, unnatural. She checked the clock: 5 p.m. Way too early for sunset.

Thick, bruised clouds rolled low on the horizon, heavy with rain and something electric. Harper's hands gripped the steering wheel with quiet force.

"Do you see that?" she asked, her voice low and tense.

Connor looked up from his phone. His relaxed expression shifted instantly. He opened his weather app, thumb flicking fast across the screen.

"Storm's coming in hard. Heavy rain, thunder, wind—it's all heading straight for us." He stared out the windshield, jaw set. "Maybe just a few minutes."

Harper's eyes scanned the road ahead, which was narrow,

winding, and had no shoulder to speak of. "Can we detour?"

Connor dragged a finger across the GPS map. "No other road for miles." He turned toward her. "You want me to take the wheel?"

"I've got it," she said too quickly, stubbornness bleeding into fear.

"Okay," he said, gently. "But if that changes, say the word and I'll drive."

She nodded, white-knuckled. The clouds rolled in darker before rain hit sharp and suddenly, as if the heavens cracked open all at once.

Harper switched on the headlights and hazards. The wipers swiped furiously, but the world beyond the glass softened into gray chaos. The road disappeared beneath rushing sheets of water.

She moved forward in her seat to see through a shower of rain. Harper clenched her jaw as she moved slowly down the road, praying she wouldn't crash into anything. The minutes dragged on as the rain kept coming down with no shine of slowing. Then suddenly, a jagged bolt of lightning split the sky ahead, lighting up a tree for a brief moment. It was enough to witness a branch break off with a sickening crack.

"Shit!" Harper's heart pounded in her chest as the car lurched, tires sliding over slick mud. They came to a jarring stop just feet from the fallen limb.

For a moment, all they could hear was the roar of rain pounding on metal and their fast, shallow breaths.

Connor's voice cut through the storm, steady and sharp. "We can't stay here. There are too many trees. Next one could come down on top of us."

Harper scanned the road, rain washing away any clear vision.

"See anything we can go under?"

He wiped a sleeve across the fogging windshield, eyes narrowing. "There—up ahead. A car wash or a garage. Abandoned, maybe."

Harper edged the car onto the road, weaving around the splintered branch. A hundred yards later, a crumbling old car wash emerged through the downpour. Its flat concrete roof was high enough to offer cover.

She pulled under the cracked roof and turned to face the road. She exhaled as if she'd been holding her breath for miles. Connor did the same beside her.

The storm raged on outside, but its sound was muted beneath the concrete. Lightning still flared, thunder rumbling deep and close. Water poured off the roof's edges in heavy streams, encasing them in a curtain of silver.

Harper leaned closer, breath fogging the glass. The storm obscured everything beyond the car wash, but she swore under her breath as she saw a figure move ahead.

Connor looked over at her, "What's the matter?"

Harper said, "I saw something."

Ten

Day 3: A Surprise

Harper rolled down her window and leaned out, squinting through the rain at the tangled mess of branches and leaves.

"Oh my God." Her voice shot up, sharp with urgency. "That's a calf."

Connor opened his window and jerked his head around to look. Sure enough, a small, soaked figure trembled beyond the fallen tree limbs.

"Damn," he muttered. "There's probably a farm nearby."

Before he could finish the thought, Harper had stepped out the door and into the storm.

"Harper!" The downpour swallowed Connor's voice. "Get back in the car!"

She didn't stop.

The rain pummeled her, the wind slashing sideways as she waded through ankle-deep water and mud. The calf struggled beneath a tangle of heavy branches, its legs flailing weakly. Its cries were thin, frightened. Harper didn't hesitate; she couldn't. All she saw was a helpless animal and the danger pressing in from all sides.

Thunder cracked overhead. The sky flashed bright white before plunging into darkness. She pushed forward, soaked to the bone, slipping on slick pavement as she neared the animal.

At the tree line, a large cow stood motionless, letting out a low, aching sound that made Harper's heart twist. The calf's mother stood there, helpless to save her baby. The calf gave another feeble kick, and Harper dropped to her knees beside it, not caring that water soaked straight through her jeans.

"Hey, hey… I've got you," Harper murmured.

A jagged bolt split the sky, the crack instant and deafening, followed by a bone-deep rumble of thunder. The air tasted metallic, but Harper stayed focused, her hands working frantically to free the calf. She tossed branches aside, her fingers raw and numb, until only one heavy limb remained.

As she crouched to lift it, a violent crack rang out above her. Harper's head snapped up, and her breath hitched. A massive branch split from the tree, its dark silhouette hurtling straight toward her.

She froze. A split second of motionless, disbelieving terror was followed by a sharp impact slamming into her side, knocking her breathless. Harper hit the ground hard, the sting of asphalt sharp through the haze. Rain pummeled her face, and her pulse thudded in her ears. She looked up, rain clouded everything but Connor's face—wild, scared, so unlike his usual calm.

The branch crashed to the ground, exactly where she'd been a moment ago. Splinters flew, and for a split-second, neither of them moved.

Harper's senses snapped into focus. She scrambled to her feet, ignoring the ache in her hip. Her gaze darted to the calf.

It was still there, unharmed. Relief washed through Harper as she looked at Connor. She didn't have to say anything as they both heaved the final branch away. The calf struggled to its feet, wobbling before it rushed to its mother's side.

Harper watched as the mother nuzzled her baby, a warmth spreading through her despite the cold.

But reality crashed in as Connor tugged her hand, urgency in his grip. "We need to get out of here," he said, his voice almost lost in the roar of the storm.

He pulled her toward the car, both of them ducking under the concrete overhang, soaked and shivering. Harper went to the driver's side as her fingers fumbled with the handle, slick from rain. She tugged. Nothing.

A pang settled in her ribs.

She yanked the handle again, harder this time. Nothing. The door didn't so much as rattle.

"Connor?" Her voice cracked under the weight of panic.

He was already circling to the other side, checking the doors with increasing urgency. When he reached hers again, he slammed his palm against the driver's window, eyes scanning the interior.

His jaw locked. "No. No, no, no."

Harper followed his gaze, and then her stomach dropped.

Sitting squarely on the center console were the keys.

And both of their phones.

Cold nausea knotted in her gut. "I–I must've hit the lock by accident..."

Connor went still. Rain dripped from his hair, and his t-shirt clung to him as he planted his hands on the car, and for a beat, Harper prepared herself for him to snap.

For a second, his jaw flexed, but he exhaled slowly, his shoulders sagging in defeat.

"It's okay," he said, wiping water from his face. "You did the right thing back there."

She stared at him, stunned. "You're seriously not mad?"

A crooked smile pulled at his lips. "What kind of asshole gets mad about saving a baby cow?"

Relief rushed through Harper, so fast and deep it made her lightheaded. She laughed, a mix of nerves and gratitude. She couldn't handle the guilt of being responsible for one more detour on this trip.

They circled the car once more, trying every door, pressing every button they could find. Nothing. Trapped.

Harper leaned against the concrete wall, soaked to the bone, the cold sinking deep into her bones. "The calf has to belong to a nearby farm. When the rain lets up, we can walk, see if anyone's home, maybe borrow a phone."

Connor stepped beside her, shoulder brushing hers. "You do realize that's how every horror movie starts, don't you?"

She gave him a sideways look. "Please. Your grumpy energy alone could scare off any serial killer."

He laughed—an actual, full laugh that warmed her more than anything else could have in the cold rain.

They stood there, both watching the downpour, neither saying a word. Harper wandered a few steps toward the edge of the shelter, arms wrapped around herself, trembling.

Connor followed. Without a word, his arms circled her from behind, solid and warm, his chest a welcome heat against her chilled skin.

She let out a breath she didn't know she'd been holding.

"Thank you," she murmured, voice rough from cold and adrenaline. "This… helps."

His chin rested lightly on her head. "Good."

For a little while, the storm wasn't so loud. The cold wasn't quite so biting.

The rain softened into a steady rhythm.

Connor's voice rumbled near her ear. "Want to sit for a bit?"

Harper barely moved, her body trembling from the cold as she silently agreed. They slid down the wall together, shoulder to shoulder, knees brushing. Connor wrapped an arm around her, pulling her close. She let herself sink into the warmth of his hold, the storm a distant hum compared to the steady rhythm of his breathing.

The rain's tempo slowed, no longer pounding hard on the pavement. Harper leaned forward, peering into the gray haze. As she relaxed, Connor watched her, his expression unreadable.

"Hey," he said, his voice a gentle pull.

She met his eyes. "Hi."

Connor's hand cupped her chin, fingers a little unsteady. Harper's breath hitched. Before she could think, he closed the space between them, his lips brushing softly over hers.

She felt the split in his lip—the rough edge of it—a jolt of memory from the fight the night before. He flinched slightly, but didn't pull away.

The kiss was gentle at first, tentative, but something shifted. It deepened, and Harper felt everything else fall away. The cold, the wet, the locked car; nothing else mattered.

The world shrank to the warmth of his mouth, the weight of his hand at the back of her neck. She moved instinctively, straddling his lap, and they both laughed, a breathless, shaky sound before their lips found each other again. Somewhere in the back of her mind, a voice screamed *terrible idea,* but her heart didn't care. Connor's hands slid along her spine, anchoring her—and for a moment, safety settled over her.

But she pulled away, breathing unevenly. The familiar flicker of doubt crept in, cold and sharp.

"What's wrong?" Connor asked, furrowing his brow.

She hesitated. "I can't do this if tomorrow you're going to pretend none of it meant anything."

His head sank, a weary breath slipping out. "I'm sorry. I don't… I'm not good at this. Every time I get close to something good, I start counting down to when it falls apart."

She leaned in, her hands cupping his face, thumbs gently tracing his cheek, the leftover bruise from the fight. That's when her eyes landed once more on the scar.

"How'd you get this?" she asked, gently tracing the faint line across his cheekbone.

Connor went still for a moment before finally looking away. "Family member of a patient. The one I lost during surgery."

Harper's breath caught. "They attacked you?"

"It was outside the hospital. I guess they needed someone to blame. I didn't fight back. Didn't feel like I could. Part of me figured I deserved it." His voice was soft, but the bitterness underneath cut deep.

Harper pressed her forehead to his. "I'm sorry that happened."

He nodded slightly, and her eyes drifted down to the outside of his right arm—another scar, more jagged.

"And this one?" she asked.

Connor let out a breath that was half a chuckle. "That was college. Bar fight. Some guy got handsy with my girlfriend at the time. I got between them, and a bottle came between me and the guy."

Harper gave a smile. "You have a bit of a hero streak."

He raised an eyebrow. "Reckless streak, maybe. I've never been good at standing by when someone was in trouble. Even when it was a terrible idea."

"Still counts."

Harper nestled her head into his chest. The steady, solid rhythm of his heartbeat beneath her ear grounded her, each beat a tether pulling her from the edge. Connor's left arm wrapped around her waist, drawing her closer, while his right hand moved in slow, soothing circles over her back. She knew better than to let herself hope. This moment might not mean more than comfort in the aftermath of chaos, but for now, she let herself sink into it. Let herself feel safe.

Eventually, the rain began to ease, the roar softening to a gentle patter. Harper slowly pulled away from Connor. Her limbs felt stiff, her skin prickled with cold, but the warmth of Connor's arm still lingered on her.. When she looked at him, there was a flicker of something in his eyes— sadness, maybe, or something heavier. She didn't ask. Instead, she stood, brushing mud from her jeans, and stepped to the edge of the car wash to check the road. Connor joined her a moment later, silent at her side. Neither of them mentioned the kiss. Or the way it had felt to hold each other.

"There," Connor said, pointing into the distance. "A farm."

Harper squinted, spotting a white farmhouse and a red barn tucked along the horizon. It was still a few miles off, but it was something.

"Let's go."

With one last glance at the car, they set off. The muddy field sucked at their shoes, each step a wet squelch. The air between them bristled with everything unsaid until Harper broke it.

"You know… making a mistake doesn't mean you have to punish yourself forever."

Connor hesitated, jaw muscles twitching. When he spoke, his voice came out clipped. "It wasn't missing a meeting. Someone died because of me."

Harper's fingers curled into her sleeves. Her voice rose, thin with frustration. "But how many people lived because of you? You didn't do it on purpose. You spent so much of your time trying to save people."

He shook his head. "It's not that simple."

"No, it's not. But if you don't figure out how to forgive yourself, you're going to stay stuck. And you're going to be miserable forever."

His shoulders went rigid. "Stop trying to fix me."

"I'm not," she said. "I think you deserve better than this… whatever this is."

His gaze didn't waver as he finally said, "Maybe if you followed your own advice, you wouldn't be running away to California."

Harper stopped walking, her pulse spiking. "Excuse me?"

Connor looked fully at her, something dark behind his eyes. "You said you weren't trying to fix me, but you're not exactly facing your mess either."

She stared at him, rain dripping from her hair. "I'm not running from Nate. I'm getting away from someone who tried to control me. Who made me feel small every single day. There's a difference."

His mouth opened, then closed. He wanted to say something else, but held back.

"I'm trying to start over," she added, voice low. "That's not the same as letting the past hold me down."

They stood there in the storm-drenched field, breathing hard, both a little stunned by how far the conversation had gone.

Without a word, she turned and continued toward the farmhouse, her footsteps heavy. Connor followed, but neither of them spoke another word.

By the time they reached the farmhouse, Harper's teeth chattered, her breath clouding in the chilled air. The white house loomed ahead. It looked like a relic from another time with a sagging wraparound porch and wooden railings bending under years of wear. Wind chimes clinked softly in the breeze, their melancholic tones mingling with the rhythmic drip of rainwater from the eaves. Nearby, the red barn stood stoic, faint shapes of animals stirring inside.

Connor moved with purpose, his boots heavy in the muck, as he went up the porch and knocked firmly on the door. Harper lingered behind him, hugging herself to fend off the biting cold, shivering despite her attempts to stay warm. She couldn't remember the last time she'd knocked on a stranger's door. Had it been when she was a kid, playing in the neighborhood? When a knock meant Halloween candy or the comfort of a friend's home, not this uncertainty.

No answer. The world was still except for the sound of stray water droplets gently tapping the earth. Connor knocked once more, this time with more urgency.

Harper's pulse quickened, the unease creeping in, an unsettling chill deeper than the cold of the storm. Her eyes darted to the mist-covered fields behind them, her thoughts drifting to the distance between here and safety. As the silence threatened to suffocate her, the door creaked open.

A man stood in the doorway, a broad silhouette outlined by

the dim light inside. Salt-and-pepper hair clung damply to his temples, his sun-darkened skin creased with years of work and weather. He was slightly shorter than Connor but held himself with an undeniable air of calm authority. His voice was steady and warm as he spoke, carrying the reassurance of someone accustomed to weathering storms.

"Can I help you?" he asked, his tone unruffled by the sudden appearance of strangers on his doorstep.

Connor opened his mouth to speak, but before he could, a voice sliced through the rain-soaked air.

"Connor? Is that you?"

Eleven

Day 3: The Stay

Harper spun around as a woman cut through the mist. Long, dark hair braided with infuriating perfection. Overalls that clung in a way no one's overalls should. The woman's eyes, large and chestnut-brown, were wide with surprise.

"Allison?" Connor's voice cracked, and Harper felt the sharp sting beneath her skin.

"Oh my gosh, Connor!" Allison dropped the basket she was carrying, half-filled with fresh eggs, and quickly came up to Connor and threw her arms around him. Connor stood stiffly at first, his arms hovering in mid-air before settling, awkwardly, around her.

Harper froze, her body plunging into icy stillness. She didn't move, didn't breathe. Her fingers curled into the soaked fabric of her sleeves until her knuckles ached.

The older man's expression shifted, his brow knitting. "Allison, you know him?"

Allison pulled away, her cheeks flushed, and turned to her father. "Yeah, Dad. This is Connor. We, uh, dated a little while ago."

Her father's face darkened, a cloud passing over his kind features. "This Connor? The one who broke your heart?"

A tiny, breathy laugh escaped Allison as she swatted his shoulder. "Dad, stop. It was a mutual breakup."

Connor's shoulders stiffened, his eyes darting to Harper, who remained motionless.

"Yeah," he muttered. "Mutual."

But Harper saw the fleeting shadow that crossed Allison's face. She clearly didn't believe her lie.

"What are you doing here?" Allison's voice was pointed as she looked between Connor and Harper, but Harper heard the undercurrent: what was he doing here, with another woman?

"We were caught in the rain a few hours ago," Connor said, his voice regaining its steadiness. "Locked the keys and our phones in the car. We were hoping to use a phone to call someone for help."

Allison's dad's face softened with understanding. "Of course. Come in, get out of the rain. I know a guy who can unlock it for you."

Connor's relief was palpable. "Thank you. We appreciate it."

Allison stepped forward, her eyes flicking between Connor and Harper. "It's late. You should both stay. Dry clothes, hot food. It's the least we can do."

But Harper heard what wasn't said, *and figure out what the hell you're doing with him.*

The idea of dry clothes and a hot meal was undeniably tempting, but the thought of spending the night under the same roof as Allison made Harper's insides twist.

Connor hesitated as he looked from Allison to Harper. "I don't know. We don't want to inconvenience you. We only need to get the car unlocked."

Allison's father spoke next, his voice calm and reassuring. "You're not inconveniencing us. Roads out here turn dangerous after a bad storm."

Connor looked toward Harper, his expression unreadable. "Can I talk to Harper for a second?"

Allison's mouth pulled together, but she gave a nod. "Of course." Without another word, she turned, picked up her basket, and followed her father inside.

Connor waited until the door clicked shut behind them before turning to Harper. They stood under the porch's overhang as the dewy aftermath of the storm hung around them.

"Are you okay with this?" he asked, his voice low. "We don't have to stay."

Harper hesitated as she looked towards the dark horizon, where thick clouds still loomed. "It's not what I want," she said. "But they're not wrong. It's safer than driving at this point."

Connor's jaw tensed. "Fine. We'll stay. But we leave first thing in the morning."

She nodded. "The earlier, the better."

Connor turned toward the door, but Harper lingered behind. Through the window, she could see Allison in the kitchen, taking the eggs out of the basket. She looked relaxed and comfortable, pretty much the exact opposite of how Harper was feeling at the moment.

Harper didn't know what was going on between Connor and Allison. She only knew the cold, and the wet, and the way Connor had hesitated when Allison hugged him—as if part of him had slipped into a different life.

They stepped into the house, warm air curling around them, thick and comforting. Harper hovered near the doorway, unsure where to put herself, while Connor looked over at Allison as she walked over to the entryway.

"Thanks for the offer," he said. "We'll stay the night."

Allison lit up as her father entered the room. "I called my friend. He should be able to get your car unlocked."

Connor stepped forward to shake his hand. "Appreciate it, sir."

The older man acknowledged them quietly, his eyes shifting between Harper and Allison, reading something Harper wished wasn't so obvious.

"Rick," the man corrected with a friendly nod. "No 'sir' around here."

"Rick," Connor echoed.

Allison eyed their dripping clothes. "You guys need to get out of those before you catch a cold." She looked at her dad. "Can Connor borrow something of yours?"

Connor shook his head. "I can wait. We'll grab clothes from the car."

Rick waved him off. "Nonsense. Might be a while. No reason to stay soaked. We'll toss your clothes in the dryer."

"And my mom should be here soon," Allison added, turning to Harper. "She won't mind if you borrow something of hers. She's short like you."

Harper arched a brow. Was that a jab or Allison being Allison? The sideways glance Connor gave her said he wasn't sure either. Harper forced a smile. "That'd be great. Thanks."

Allison beckoned for them to follow her and Harper took in the kitchen as they walked through. It carried the warm scent of cinnamon and aged wood. Scuffed hardwood stretched beneath their feet, polished carefully despite the wear. Honey-toned cabinets glowed under soft yellow light. A kettle whistled softly on the stove, steam fogging the windows.

Ahead, the living room hugged the staircase—a worn leather couch sagged near a stone fireplace cluttered with framed photos and a flickering candle. Blankets lay folded over an armchair, and a bookcase stood near the window, heavy with well-thumbed volumes.

Allison led them upstairs, footsteps light on the creaking wooden floor. In what had to be her parents' room, she rifled through drawers, pulling out a pair of jeans and a soft navy t-shirt. "Shower's there," she said to Connor, nodding toward the bathroom.

"Thanks," Connor said, glancing briefly at Harper before disappearing inside.

The moment the door clicked shut, Allison's smile evaporated. She looked through another drawer and tossed a pair of sweatpants and an oversized t-shirt at Harper without a word. Caught off guard, Harper barely caught them.

"Uh… thanks?"

Allison's tone turned sharp. "You can use the shower downstairs. Follow me."

They reached the halfway point on the staircase when Harper caught the way Allison's posture stiffened, the temperature in the stairwell dropping a few degrees before she even opened her mouth. Allison suddenly turned, her voice low and loaded. "So, you and Connor—you're together?"

Harper stopped, taken aback by the acid in her tone. "We're not dating. We happen to be sharing a car on the way to California."

Allison's lips curled into a smirk. She jabbed a finger at Harper. "Well, don't bother trying anything. We might be broken up, but I'm going to have Connor again."

Harper's voice dropped, calm but cold. "Get your finger out of my face."

Allison's smug look faltered. Without another word, she yanked the clothes out of Harper's hands. "Guess there aren't any extra clothes after all."

She turned and strode up the stairs, leaving Harper standing there feeling damp and irritated.

Let her play her petty little games. Harper had survived worse than a jealous ex with a superiority complex. She looked up and down the staircase before deciding there was no point in lingering. She wasn't about to give Allison the satisfaction of seeing her rattled, so she made her way into the kitchen.

Rick stood at the stove, stirring a large pot that filled the air with the mouthwatering scent of garlic and herbs. He looked over his shoulder when he heard Harper and grinned.

"Allison find you something to change into? You look about one sneeze away from a cold."

Harper forced a smile. "She's, uh… working on it."

Rick's expression softened as if he saw straight through her but chose not to press. "Want to help with dinner?"

Relieved for something to do, Harper perked up. "Definitely. What can I do?"

He handed her a garlic bulb and a knife. "How are you with garlic?"

"Skilled enough not to lose a finger," she joked, rolling up her damp sleeves.

She got to work, grateful for the distraction. Upstairs, the shower was running. Connor, no doubt, was enjoying the warmth Harper could only dream about. A flicker of envy passed through her as she tried not to shiver.

She didn't notice Rick leave until he returned, holding out a thick, oversized sweater.

"Here. Toss this on before you freeze solid."

Surprised, she set the knife down and pulled the sweater over her head. It felt so soft and smelled faintly of detergent and wood smoke.

"Thank you," she said, voice sincere.

Rick gave her a kind smile before returning to the stove. Harper brought over the chopped garlic, which he tossed into a sizzling pan with olive oil, Parmesan, and a squeeze of lemon. The kitchen bloomed with warmth and scent.

"Thanks for doing all this for us," she said as she rested her elbows on the counter.

Rick gave a modest shrug. "Helping folks in trouble is what we're about."

She met his eyes for a moment before responding. "Still. It means a lot."

Before Rick could say anything else, footsteps creaked on the stairs.

Connor reappeared, with Allison following close behind. His brown hair was still damp, his face freshly washed, but the scruff framing his jaw only sharpened the rugged edge of his looks. The borrowed navy shirt draped neatly over his broad frame, and though the jeans weren't quite his size, it didn't matter. If anything, the imperfect fit only made him look better.

The soft cotton clung to his shoulders, hinting at his muscles beneath, and the faded denim rode low on his hips in a way that made Harper's breath catch.

He looked devastatingly good.

Harper didn't mean to stare, but her gaze lingered a moment too long.

Snapping back to reality, Harper caught sight of Allison, who was watching her intently. The firm set of her mouth and the cold gleam in her eyes made it clear she hadn't missed a thing.

Connor's voice broke through the moment as he eyed Harper. "You get a shower yet?"

Harper shook her head, but Rick jumped in before she could answer. "Allison's getting her some clothes."

Allison paused but recovered quickly. "I checked… but my mom didn't have anything that would fit."

Harper tilted her head, dry. "That's okay. I'll shower and hang out in a towel while my clothes dry. No big deal."

She didn't miss the flicker of amusement that crossed Connor's face before he smothered it.

As Harper pushed off the counter to leave the room, Allison spun around.

"Actually, I forgot to check one more spot. Be right back."

She darted upstairs. Harper smirked. At least now Allison would have to work a little harder to keep up the act.

The front door creaked open, and a woman stepped inside, brushing rain from her sleeves. Her coat was damp, streaked with bits of hay and mud. She paused, her eyes sweeping over Harper and Connor with a flicker of surprise. Before she could say anything, Rick stepped in beside her.

"Hi, Ellen. These are a couple of Allison's acquaintances, Connor and Harper. Got caught out in the storm."

Ellen exhaled, peeling off her gloves. "Oh, hello there. I'm glad you're both okay; it's a mess out there. I've been in the barn half the afternoon. One of the calves wandered off with her mama, and they showed up soaked through."

Connor straightened. "Was she a little brown one, with a white patch on her nose?"

Ellen shifted her attention to him. "Yes! You saw her?"

Harper added. "She was stuck and crying in the mud, and we were able to pull her out."

Surprise flickered across Ellen's face before it melted into a grateful smile. "That was you two? Lord, we didn't even realize she was missing until I went to check on the rest of the animals. You might've saved her life."

Connor shrugged, but Harper could see the hint of warmth behind his otherwise casual posture.

"We were only trying to help," she said, brushing a damp strand of hair behind her ear.

Footsteps echoed on the stairs, and Allison appeared holding a bundle of clothes. Ellen turned, her smile growing wider.

"I'm glad we're able to return the favor." She said to Connor and Harper, "You'll both be lucky if you don't catch a chill."

Harper took the clothes from Allison with a simple "Thanks," as Allison handed them over with a glance that was anything but warm.

Harper excused herself from the group and made her way upstairs to the bathroom.

Once inside, Harper examined the clothes Allison had handed her—an oversized, old t-shirt and saggy sweatpants clearly chosen to maximize frump. Harper let out a chuckle and shook her head. If this was Allison's idea of sabotage, Harper had survived worse. A little frump wouldn't break her.

After a quick shower, Harper slipped into the baggy clothes. Wearing them without underwear or a bra felt strange and vaguely vulnerable, but putting on damp underthings seemed worse.

She paused at the mirror. Her reflection didn't show the strain of the day, nor the way bitterness sat so openly on Allison's face. Still, unease clung to Harper. How would Connor act around Allison now that they were under the same roof? Would this give them a chance to reconnect? The idea made Harper's stomach turn, and she hated how much it mattered to her.

After one final glance in the mirror, she turned and headed downstairs.

In the kitchen, Ellen was plating food while Connor sat at the table. He looked up as Harper entered, and his eyes lingered for a second before flicking back to his plate. Allison sat next to him, posture perfect, eyes smug.

"You can toss your wet stuff in the dryer," Ellen said kindly. "It's off the kitchen. Connor's are already in there."

"Thanks," Harper said, her voice steady.

She crossed the room, ignoring Allison's stare, and stepped into the laundry room. She added her clothes to the dryer, along with Rick's damp sweater, and started the cycle, letting the warm hum fill the room. When she returned, a steaming plate of pasta waited for her.

She sat and took her first bite, and nearly groaned out loud. Warm, garlicky, bright with lemon. Her second helping came quickly.

Halfway through, Allison's voice sliced through the easy rhythm of forks on plates.

"Wow, you're going for it. Must *really* love carbs."

Harper didn't look up. She calmly chewed her bite, swallowed, and replied, "I do. They're kind of essential for survival."

Across the table, Connor coughed into his drink, eyes dancing. Allison wasn't amused.

Rick's phone buzzed, cutting through the moment. He picked

it up with a brisk, "Yeah?" After a short exchange, he hung up and turned to them. "That was my buddy. He'll be here in a few to give you a lift to the car."

Connor responded with a sincere, "Thanks again. Seriously, that's a huge help."

"I'll come with you," Harper offered, trying to keep her tone casual, even though it felt anything but.

But Connor gave a slight shake of his head. "It's okay. I'll bring the car here so we can head out early."

She shifted uneasily, the dread settling deeper. The thought of being left alone with Allison made her want to crawl under the floorboards.

A few minutes later, a knock at the door signaled that Rick's friend had arrived. The man had a kind, weathered face and offered a warm smile as he stepped inside.

Connor stood up and exchanged a quick look with Harper before heading out. The door closed behind him with a click, and suddenly the room felt too still.

Harper found herself finishing up her dinner while making polite conversation with Ellen—who, thankfully, was as sweet and easygoing as ever. Allison, on the other hand, made no effort to have a conversation, and she seemed to interrupt whenever Harper spoke.

It was going to be a long wait.

As the women finished up their dinner, Ellen turned to Harper. "Let's figure out sleeping arrangements."

She glanced toward Allison, a flicker of uncertainty in her eyes. "We have a guest room that'll fit both of you."

Harper caught the subtle hesitation and decided to clear the air. "We're not, um, together like that. I'm fine taking the couch if that's easier."

Allison's smirk twitched, and Harper's lips pressed together, but Ellen smiled warmly.

"You don't have to take the couch. I'll get the guest room upstairs ready for you, and Connor can take the couch down here."

"Thank you," Harper said. "Really. Is there anything I can do to help?"

"Nope," Ellen said, waving her off. "You relax. You've had a rough day."

Harper glanced at Allison, who looked as if she wanted to ask something, maybe dig deeper, but thought better of it and silently left the room to help her mom. Harper closed her eyes briefly, bracing for the strange tension. Being in someone else's home was always a little awkward. Being in your sort-of love interest's ex's family home? That was a new level of weirdness.

She stayed there for a moment, unsure what to do with herself. Fidgeting wouldn't help. After a glance around, she decided to clean up the kitchen. It was the least she could do to repay some of Rick and Ellen's kindness.

By the time Harper finished drying the last dish, the front door opened. Connor stepped inside, bags slung over one shoulder and his suitcase in hand. Rick followed closely, carrying Harper's suitcase. The tension within Harper softened the second she saw him. She smiled instinctively, and when Connor's eyes landed on hers, his answering smile made her stomach do flip-flops.

He kicked off his shoes and set the bags down. Rick muttered something about finding Ellen and disappeared into the house.

Connor watched him go, then turned to Harper, running his hands through his hair. "I still can't believe we're staying at Allison's parents' house."

Harper gave a small laugh as she slid a dish into the cabinet. "Honestly? It kind of feels on-brand for this whole trip."

Connor smirked. "I have to tell you—"

She leaned in, pulse skipping. But before Connor could finish, the clack of Allison's footsteps on the tile cut through the air. Her eyes darted between them with a flicker of suspicion.

"The couch is all set for you, Connor." The fake sweetness in Allison's voice was so thick that Harper was amazed no one else choked on it. She turned to Harper, her face hardening as if it hurt to show kindness. "And you're upstairs in the guest bedroom."

Connor inclined his head slightly. "Thanks, Allison."

The glow on Allison's face at his gratitude made Harper want to gag. A fresh wave of irritation prickled up Harper's spine. Nope. She was done with this situation.

"Thanks," Harper said curtly, crossing the room to grab her clothes from the dryer. She scooped up her bag, grabbed her suitcase, and headed out of the kitchen before anyone could say anything else.

She passed Allison's parents in the living room on her way to the stairs. Ellen looked up from the coffee table, a deck of cards in one hand and a folded blanket tucked under her arm.

"Oh, Harper," she said, blinking as if something had just occurred to her. "Did you do the dishes?"

Harper paused on the steps. "Yeah. I figured it was the least I could do."

Ellen's face softened, genuinely touched. "Thank you, sweetheart. I was busy getting the couch and guest bedroom ready and completely forgot about them."

Harper shrugged, a little shy under the praise. "No problem. It gave me something to do."

Ellen smiled warmly. "We're setting up for a quick game of cards; do you want to join us?"

Harper paused. She was mentally fried, and the last thing she wanted was to make more awkward small talk. But Connor stepped into the room, with Allison practically attached to his side. Harper caught the amused glance Ellen gave her daughter.

Connor looked at Harper, and she silently pleaded with her eyes: *don't make me stay down here.* For a brief second, she wondered if he'd pick up on it.

He did.

He gave her a knowing look, his mouth starting to form a response until Allison cut in, too brightly.

"Yeah, it'll be fun. A little competition never hurt anyone."

Harper shot a look at Connor and caught the annoyed exhale she now easily recognized. But, she wasn't the type to shy away from a challenge, especially not when it came from Allison.

She hesitated only a moment before plastering on a smile. "Sure. Why not? Let me put my stuff in the room first." Connor gave her a long look before she turned and made her way up the stairs.

When Harper returned, everyone was gathered around the coffee table in the living room. A warm table lamp cast golden light over a scattered deck of worn playing cards and mismatched bowls of popcorn Ellen had set out. Rain tapped gently against the windows, a soft and steady rhythm. It should've been comforting, but to Harper, it sounded like static in a room full of landmines.

Allison sat next to Connor, *too* close, and Harper took the spot between Ellen and Rick, trying not to read too much into the arrangement.

The first few rounds passed in easy conversation. Harper let herself breathe, lulled by the rhythm of the game and Ellen's warm laughter. But then Allison opened her mouth.

"Oh, *Connor*," she said with a syrupy laugh, dropping a hand of cards on the table. "Remember that weekend in the Catskills? When we played this game, and you kept losing miserably?"

Connor gave a small, unreadable smile. "Barely. You always made up your own rules."

"You didn't understand them," she said, nudging him playfully with her elbow as if the whole exchange was a sweet inside joke between them.

Harper looked down at her cards, her mouth pressing into a thin line. She didn't need to look up to know Allison's eyes were on her, practically glowing with satisfaction.

Later, when Harper made a risky move and dropped a queen, Allison raised her eyebrows. "Bold move." She offered a tight, clearly forced smile. "Interesting strategy, but... well, you don't exactly have a poker face."

Harper returned the smile with one of her own, all teeth and ice. "It's more fun when you don't play it safe."

Rick chuckled, missing the subtext entirely. "That's the spirit."

The conversation looped through travel stories, old high school memories, weird relatives, and somehow, every topic seemed to give Allison another chance to insert herself. Another opportunity to remind Harper how much *history* she and Connor shared.

When Harper offered a lighthearted story from the road trip, Allison didn't miss a beat.

"Oh, that reminds me of when Connor and I got lost outside Nashville," she cut in, voice sweet with just enough edge. "Remember, Con? You ditched the GPS for whatever that sketchy gas station guy told you."

Harper clasped her hands firmly in her lap beneath the table. Connor didn't say anything. He didn't correct her. Didn't shift away when Allison leaned into him for the millionth time.

She told herself not to care. Still, every second Connor didn't speak up scraped at her nerves.

Every one of Allison's comments was small and technically harmless, but Harper could feel the bite beneath the sugar. The intention was clear. And judging by the glances Ellen exchanged with Rick across the table, Harper wasn't the only one who noticed. Still, no one said anything.

Maybe this was… Allison.

Harper stared down at her cards, the numbers swimming uselessly in front of her. She'd known from the moment they arrived that staying here wouldn't be easy. What she hadn't expected was how *isolated* she'd feel; how much it would sting to be the outsider in a room full of shared history and inside jokes between Allison and Connor.

It hit her all at once.

She was more of a stranger to Connor than anyone else at this table.

And somehow, *that* hurt the most.

The final hand came around. Ellen clapped her hands together. "Another round?"

"I think I'm going to call it a night," Harper said, rising from her seat. "Long day."

She kept her voice polite. Only Connor seemed to notice the tremor behind it. Harper turned to Allison's parents and added sincerely, "Thanks a lot. You've been really kind."

Ellen and Rick returned her smile with genuine warmth, and Harper wondered—not for the first time—how two such decent people had raised someone as sharp-edged as Allison.

She barely spared Allison a glance but held Connor's eyes for a beat. His mouth parted, hesitation flickering across his face, but she didn't give him the chance. She turned and headed up the stairs.

She was halfway to the guest room when soft footsteps echoed behind her.

"Harper. Wait."

She paused, glancing over her shoulder.

Connor stood a few steps down the staircase, his hands at his sides. He didn't move, but stayed close enough that their eyes were nearly level.

"I just…" He hesitated. "I wanted to say goodnight. And to check if you were okay."

Her brows lifted, disbelief edging into her voice. "I'm fantastic, thanks for asking. Nothing beats a room full of petty digs and passive aggression to end a perfect night."

He blinked, clearly not expecting the bite.

Harper let out a short, dry laugh and turned away. "Goodnight."

She had barely taken a step when his hand gently caught her wrist.

"What are you doing?" she snapped, yanking her arm. "I'm going to bed."

He released her instantly, his voice low. Steady, but laced with something rougher underneath. "I'm sorry. About tonight. All of it. I know it was uncomfortable."

She stared at him, emotions swirling. "I can handle uncomfortable," she said, her voice steady but sharp. "I can even handle being the outsider. But what I can't handle is sitting there while someone throws digs at me, and the one person who I thought was kind of a friend… doesn't say anything."

Connor's usual composure cracked. "I should've said something, but I didn't want to start a scene. Not in front of her parents."

Harper let out a bitter laugh. "Yeah, because God forbid you upset Allison." Her eyes flashed. "She's your ex, and we both know she's not ready to stay that way."

Connor looked stunned for a second, speechless. Harper turned on her heel and took a step, throwing a parting shot over her shoulder. "Good luck with that, Connor."

But he wasn't finished. Connor closed the gap between them in two strides, now standing a step above her. Harper was close to him, too close to those brown eyes that seemed to see more than she wanted them to.

"This isn't a game," he said, his voice rough. "I want nothing to do with Allison. That chapter's over. I'm not going back."

The words sparked between them, but Harper didn't flinch. "Is it?" she said coldly. "You've known her for over a year. Me? I'm the girl you're stuck in a car with. A couple of hotel rooms and a few inside jokes don't change that."

Connor recoiled as if she'd physically shoved him. "You know that's not how I see you."

She kept her arms at her side, curling her fingers until her nails bit into her skin. "Could've fooled me. You've been giving me emotional whiplash ever since we left New York. I have no idea where I stand with you, and I'm done twisting myself into knots trying to figure it out."

He opened his mouth to respond, but she cut him off. "Let's stop this before it turns into something messier than it already is. You and Allison have history. You and I… don't. That's all there is to it."

She turned and started up the stairs, but he called after her one more time. "Harper."

She stopped and cast a tired glance his way. He seemed about to say more, maybe even step closer, but she raised a hand to stop him.

"I really don't feel good about being here. And I want to forget tonight happened before I start regretting this whole road trip."

Before he could answer, she turned and walked the rest of the way to the guest room. The door clicked softly shut behind her.

Harper slumped by the door and let out a heavy sigh, grateful for the solitude. She'd felt some kind of connection to Connor over the past couple of days, but now, with the weight of everything pressing down on her, she found herself questioning it all. And it stung more than she expected. Harper shook her head, trying to clear the spiraling thoughts before pushing herself off the door and reaching for her pajamas in her suitcase.

Even as she went through the familiar motions of getting ready for bed, her thoughts kept drifting to Connor. She couldn't shake the nagging feeling that Allison was right: Connor was pulled toward her, whether he wanted to admit it or not. It wasn't subtle—the way Allison watched him, clung to him. She wasn't about to let this chance slip away.

Harper clenched her jaw so hard it ached. She hated that she couldn't stop herself from wondering if it was inevitable. She knew, all too well, how easy it was to fall into old patterns with an ex, especially when there was comfort in the familiarity of the past. But that didn't mean it felt any better.

Exhaustion weighed her down, heavy as lead, but her mind refused to quiet. She sank into the guest bed, the soft sheets folding around her, almost dragging her under. Her eyes fluttered shut, searching for peace.

But sleep didn't last.

A branch brushed the window in steady taps, dragging Harper out of a light doze. Her mouth felt dry—cottony, parched—like she hadn't had a sip of water in hours. When she saw the time on her phone: 1:30 am, she gave up on trying to fall back asleep. With a groan, she swung her legs over the side of the bed and padded softly downstairs in search of a glass of water.

Moving quietly, Harper almost reached the bottom step and paused. Low voices floated up from the living room, too soft to hear but intimate in a way that made Harper's skin crawl. She edged closer, peeking around the corner, her heart pounding hard in her chest.

Connor stood by the couch with Allison, leaning in too close. Their heads tipped together, the space between them far too small.

Harper should've turned around. She *knew* she should've turned around.

But she didn't.

Instead, Harper slowly lowered herself a bit more, straining to catch their words. Most of it faded into hushed murmurs—until one phrase cut through sharp and clear: *"I've missed you."*

She couldn't tell who had said it. Connor? Allison? It didn't matter. The effect was the same. Harper's whole body went numb.

Her eyes didn't leave the spot where Allison's hand traced the curve of Connor's arm. Harper's breath caught; the air froze in her lungs. She saw his head dip, and saw that he didn't pull away.

As if in slow motion, Allison leaned in. And kissed him. And Connor… didn't move.

Harper's vision blurred. She didn't realize she was shaking

until her damp hand slipped from the railing she'd been clinging to. A cold, hollow ache bloomed in her chest and spread fast, consuming her. She stumbled upstairs, barely aware of her surroundings, driven by pure instinct.

Once in the bedroom, she shut the door without a sound and collapsed onto the bed. Her pillow caught the first hot tear before she could stop it. The kiss replayed a cruel, unrelenting loop. Allison leaning in. Connor not stopping her.

Harper's jaw clenched, fingers knotting in the bedsheet.

Stupid. Weak. Predictable.

How had she let herself fall into this? How had she let herself believe, even for a second, that she meant something more to him?

More tears came, angry and hot. Harper buried her face deeper into the pillow, holding in sobs that still managed to escape in trembling gasps.

Of course, Allison wasn't finished. Of course, Connor hadn't truly moved on.

Harper wanted to scream, to run downstairs and cause a scene. But she stayed put, raw and fragile, letting the pain carve her empty.

The night dragged on, thick with tension. Sleep didn't come easy. It hovered, splintered and shallow, broken by the thoughts Harper couldn't keep out.

Twelve

Day 4: Confessions

She must have drifted off at some point, though it hardly felt like rest. Morning slipped in through the blinds, soft and uninvited, a sliver of light brushing across her face. For one blissful, treacherous second, Harper forgot where she was. Then it all crashed over her like a cold wave to the face: the living room, the kiss, how Connor didn't pull away.

Dread pooled all around her.

Harper stayed tucked beneath the covers, frozen in the safety of stillness, listening to the faint murmur of voices downstairs. Laughter. Footsteps. Life going on as if nothing had happened. Her throat felt dry; it was scratchy, almost raw. She swallowed hard, blaming the crying, but the faint warmth in her cheeks made her frown. Maybe it was the stress. Or lack of sleep.

A knock at the door made her flinch.

"One second!" she called, bolting upright. She jumped out of bed and went to the mirror above the dresser; her reflection made her wince—bloodshot eyes, mascara smeared beneath them in dark streaks. She scrubbed at her face, cursing herself for not waking earlier.

"It's me," Connor's voice came softly through the door.

Her pulse skittered. Instinctively, she stepped back, as though the door might open on its own.

"I'll be down soon," she said, voice clipped. "Let me get dressed."

A pause. Then: "Can I come in?"

Her fingers dug into the dresser. "No."

Connor didn't say anything more. She imagined him standing there, confused, maybe even hurt. For a moment, she thought he might keep pushing, but his footsteps soon faded down the hall.

Harper let out a shaky breath. Relief was bitter and fleeting.

She knew she was being petty. And she knew she couldn't avoid Connor forever. But all she cared about was covering the undeniable evidence of last night's crying session.

But something felt off.

A strange weight settled over her, dull and slow, as if her body was moving through molasses. She pressed a hand to her forehead and it still felt warm. Probably from the blankets. Hopefully. But her scratchy throat wasn't a good sign, and her limbs felt too heavy, her thoughts a little slow.

Great. Getting sick. Exactly what I need.

Harper dressed as simply as possible in a plain white t-shirt and denim shorts before slipping into the bathroom. She brushed her teeth, splashed her face with cold water, and applied her makeup with surgical precision. When she looked in the mirror, the damage was contained. Her eyes were still a little swollen, her skin a shade paler than usual, but she could pass for normal. Calm. Unbothered.

Downstairs, the kitchen was cozy and cheerful. A spread of bagels, cream cheese, and fruit sat on the table. Ellen smiled warmly when Harper stepped in, suitcase and bag in hand.

"Good morning!" Harper chirped, setting her things by the door.

"Come have some bagels," Ellen offered. "There's plenty."

Harper slid into an empty chair, away from both Connor and Allison, and grabbed a plain bagel, smearing it with butter. She felt his stare burning into the side of her face, but refused to meet it.

She wasn't ready to face him.

"Did you sleep okay?" Ellen asked kindly.

"I did," Harper said, lying smoothly. "The bed was comfy."

Allison's voice cut in; her voice was sugary sweet with a blade beneath. "Are you sure? You look exhausted."

Harper's jaw clenched, but her smile stayed perfectly in place. "One of the best sleeps of my life," she said breezily. "How was your night?"

A flicker of surprise crossed Allison's face. She wasn't expecting that.

"Really good," she replied, drawing out the words. "Like... *really* good."

Harper's smile didn't waver. She took a bite of her bagel, chewing slowly to keep from saying something she'd regret.

They finished breakfast and tidied up. Harper stayed busy, wiping down already clean counters, stacking plates too neatly, anything to avoid catching Connor's eye. She moved on autopilot. At some point, while Ellen and Rick chatted in the next room and Connor was distracted drying his hands, Harper slipped the car keys off the hook by the door and tucked them into her shorts' pocket. She wanted to control something—anything—at that moment.

When it was time to go, they thanked Allison's parents one last time. But Harper's heart clenched as she watched Allison wrap Connor in a hug that said *mine*. Harper turned away before she could see how he reacted, slipping out the door and into the car.

She slid into the driver's seat and shut the door with finality. The keys rattled slightly in her hand before she pushed them into the ignition.

Connor slid in beside her. "I can drive if you want," he offered, voice low.

Even that simple offer carried a sting. "No. I've got it."

"Okay."

She didn't reply. Connor turned his attention to the GPS, entering the next leg of their route. By nightfall, they were supposed to reach Arizona. That was the plan. But Harper wasn't sure where her mind was anymore; it was trapped in last night's antics, still hearing whispered words and replaying Allison and Connor's kiss on a loop.

They pulled away from the house. The road was washed out and wrecked by the storm. Fallen branches and silver puddles caught the light, sharp and fractured as broken glass. The farmhouse faded behind them.

Harper swallowed hard. She needed something to drink but water could wait. Everything could wait.

Silence settled, thick and dense. Connor was the first to crack it. "You okay?"

She didn't look at him. "I'm fine."

"You sure?"

"Yes," she snapped. "I want to get on with this trip."

He shifted, the leather of the seat whispering under his weight. "Something seems off."

Harper exhaled through her nose, a sharp and irritated sound. "I didn't sleep well."

"You told Ellen it was the best night of your life."

She flinched. "Well, I lied. Surprise."

Connor's voice stayed level. "Why couldn't you sleep?"

Harper stared ahead. "My brain wouldn't shut off. That's all."

Connor tracked her face, voice low. "What were you thinking about?"

She gave a dry, humorless laugh. "Easier to ask what I *wasn't* thinking about."

He didn't push. Not at first. When he spoke, his tone was softer. "You don't have to spiral alone, you know. You can talk to me."

She turned to him, her expression cool but brittle around the edges. "I'd honestly rather not."

That pulled a flicker of surprise from him. "Harper, I'm not going to judge you."

She gripped the steering wheel a bit harder. "I don't even really know you," she said, voice edged and low. "So no, I'm not going to crack myself open and hand you the pieces."

Connor exhaled through his nose, "I think we're beyond being simply strangers at this point."

She gave him a sideways look. "Let's not make more of this than it is, Connor. Besides, you're the one who didn't want to make this a bonding trip."

That landed between them with a quiet thud.

He looked away, gazing out the window at the passing open fields. After a moment, he asked carefully, "Does this have to do with Allison?"

A brittle pause. "No," Harper lied.

He didn't press, but she could feel the question lingering between them.

"I still can't believe she was at that farmhouse," he said.

"Crazy coincidence," Harper muttered, voice hollow. "You really never met her parents? Or knew they had a farm out here?" she asked, unable to help herself. "I thought you two dated for a while."

He didn't answer immediately. "We did. But Allison said she didn't introduce guys to her parents unless it was a serious relationship. Said they became too attached, so she never wanted me to come with her when she visited."

Harper gave a tight nod, eyes fixed ahead. "I guess that makes sense." She forced a casual tone. "Well, everything happens for a reason. Maybe fate brought us there."

He didn't respond.

"She seemed happy to see you," she added, each word dipped in venom.

Harper clocked the nervous rhythm of Connor's fingers—a tell she was getting too good at reading. "It was interesting to see her."

No explanation. No reassurance. Nothing.

Harper felt the words slice into her, clean and cruel. She opened her mouth, questions pressing at her throat, but none escaped. She couldn't bear to hear the answers.

Instead, Harper flicked on the radio. Static buzzed for a moment before giving way to a soft, melancholic melody. Music was a safer companion at this point.

They drove on in silence, the road stretching ahead in endless, empty miles. Only the steady hum of tires and the occasional rustle of wind rattled the windows.

Connor spoke after a while. "You were brave yesterday."

Harper blinked, caught off guard by his voice. "What?"

He didn't look at her as he kept his eyes on the passing landscape. "With the calf. Not everyone would've done that."

She shrugged it off, unwilling to let the warmth sneak in. "That's… kind of out of nowhere."

He shrugged, eyes still on the road. "Been thinking about it. Most people don't run into a storm for an animal."

"You did," she countered.

"Because you did first." His voice was low, thoughtful. "You didn't hesitate."

She gave a short, dry laugh. "I don't enjoy watching something suffer. That's all."

Connor watched her. "That says more about you than you think."

She looked away, feeling the weight of the compliment settle inside her. Compliments were harder to deflect when they were sincere.

"It wasn't a big deal," she said, brushing hair behind her ear. "Simply the right thing to do."

"Which most people talk about but don't actually *do*," he murmured.

Stillness fell, heavier than before.

After a pause, Connor added, "I take it you've been around people who didn't act that way."

Her mouth twisted. "You've been around Nate for more than five minutes. That was probably enough."

Connor's expression turned thoughtful. "Didn't get the sense he's big on empathy."

"He's not," she said, voice flat. "He was good at pretending, though. Especially in the beginning."

Connor's eyes found hers once more, allowing her to go through memories.

"Nate used to say things that made me question everything—my memory, my instincts, how I felt." Harper's voice was low, almost reflective. "It was never loud or dramatic. Just... off, in this subtle, insidious way. He was so good at twisting things that half the time I thought I was the one losing it."

She hesitated, struggling to keep her voice steady. "You stop trusting yourself. Little by little. That's worse than anything else."

"What made you see him for what he was?" Connor asked, gentle but direct.

She stared ahead, her voice hollow. "We were in a park. This little girl dropped her ice cream cone and started crying. Nate watched her for a second and instead of helping, he said, 'Life teaches lessons early.' As if it were a joke."

Connor didn't say anything.

"That was the moment," Harper said, her voice barely above a whisper. "I saw how cold he really was. It wasn't dramatic. But it was like someone turned on the lights."

She didn't realize she'd been holding her breath until Connor's voice cut through.

"You didn't deserve that," he said, calm and sure.

Harper glanced at him, and for once, didn't look away.

"I know," she said, "No one does. I'm hoping Nate doesn't fool another girl anytime soon."

"It's strange, isn't it?" Connor said. "How you can ignore all the big red flags... until one tiny moment shatters the illusion." She gave him a sideways glance. "Why are you bringing all this up?"

Connor ran a hand through his hair, his knuckles pale where

they clenched his knee. "I don't know. I've been thinking a lot about the past lately."

Harper let out a short, humorless laugh. "Funny. For two people trying to get away from our old lives, we sure keep tripping over them."

He gave a dry chuckle. "Yeah. What's up with that?"

Harper gave him a half-smile as she turned her face toward the window, her voice barely audible. "I believe everything happens for a reason."

Connor's lips pressed into a line. "I've never bought into that."

"How can you not?" she asked. "Look at your life—there's always a reason why things turned out the way they did."

He stared out at the dark fields rolling by. "Or maybe life's chaos. No plan. No purpose. Whatever happens, happens."

She hesitated. "So us ending up in the same car; what was that? Chaos?"

Connor opened his mouth, closed it, and looked away. "I'm still figuring that out."

Her heart twisted. The words landed harder than she expected. She realized that was pretty much the opposite of what she wanted to hear from him.

Harper hadn't meant to, but the image of Allison kissing Connor was still etched in her memory. It was a stain that refused to fade. Connor hadn't exactly pushed Allison away, and now Harper didn't want to be the girl pining for someone who might still be in love with their ex.

"Time's running out," she said suddenly.

"That's not true."

"It is." Her voice cracked. "We'll be in California soon. You'll go your way, I'll go mine. And this will become a crazy story we'll tell people at parties."

Connor faced her. "Is that what you want?"

"I don't know what I want," she whispered. "And I don't know what you want, either."

She darted a glance at him, but she wasn't sure she wanted to see the answer. But Connor wasn't looking at her; his stare was distant as he stared out the window, his fingers absentmindedly tracing the scruff on his jaw.

Harper's heart clenched. Was he thinking about Allison?

The ache in her throat deepened, raw and unfamiliar. Maybe it was emotion. Maybe it was the scratchy burn that had been building since she woke up. A warmth simmered under her skin all morning, subtle but steady, her body working harder than it should to keep up.

She blinked hard, willing the tears away. And without warning, she jerked the car toward the next exit.

Connor straightened in his seat. "Where are you going?"

"I need water," she said, too fast.

They pulled into a gas station, and as Harper stepped out, the floor tipped beneath her, her vision narrowing. She gripped the doorframe, her knuckles whitening.

Connor was beside her in an instant. "Harper?"

"I'm fine," she lied, forcing a weak smile. "I'm going to get something to drink."

Connor gave her a concerned look as he followed her inside the gas station. The harsh light made her head throb. She went to the bathroom and splashed cold water on her neck, letting the coolness bleed into her skin. When she emerged, she grabbed water and Advil.

Connor met her in the checkout line and eyed her haul. "You're getting sick."

She opened her mouth to argue, but they were next in line.

She didn't need an audience for her denial.

At the car, Connor's hand hovered over her shoulder. "Let me drive. We'll fill up and keep moving."

"Okay." Her voice lost its edge, slipping into exhaustion.

Once they were on the road again, Connor didn't let it go. "Stop pretending you're fine. What's wrong?"

"My throat hurts. My head too. And I'm… hot."

He reached over, placing his palm on her forehead. His touch was cool, but a jolt ran through her all the same. His eyes widened. "You're burning up. Why didn't you say something?"

She reclined, closing her eyes. "Because it started happening this morning. I didn't think it was a big deal."

Connor's tone turned authoritative, the doctor in him coming out. "You have to rest. We'll get a hotel in a few hours so you can sleep in a bed."

"No." Her eyes snapped open. "We have to keep moving. Time's running out."

"We'll make it." His voice was firm. "If we push through today and stop later on, we'll still be on track."

Harper's shoulders slumped, and the fight drained out of her. "Fine."

As the miles stretched on, the road wound ahead, and Harper let herself drift. But even in sleep, unease lingered.

Harper went in and out of a feverish sleep, her mind a haze of half-formed dreams and reality. At some point, she thought she felt the car stop, the rumble of the engine fading. Somewhere in the fog of fever dreams, a cool hand brushed her forehead, the scent of rain and soap cutting through the fog. She felt a blanket settle around her shoulders, a pillow beneath her cheek. Connor.

Her body shivered uncontrollably, and from time to time,

Connor's cold hand rested on her forehead or shoulder, his touch a small comfort. Time blurred until Connor slipped his arms beneath her and lifted her, strong and steady.

Harper was too feverish to register much, but the cool air brushed her skin, and fluorescent lights whirred overhead as he carried her through what she slowly realized was a hotel. When he laid her on the bed, the crisp sheets felt heavenly, and she closed her eyes, letting the relief settle in.

Connor gently pulled the blankets over her, tucking her in with surprising tenderness.

"Can I get you anything?" he asked, his voice low and soothing.

Her mouth burned with every swallow. "Something to drink. And more Advil."

He nodded. "I'll run down to the lobby. You'll be okay?"

She managed a weak wave of her hand. "Yeah."

Connor hesitated, his eyes dark with worry. Harper sat up, realizing how badly she needed to pee. She swung her legs over the bed and stood up, but the room spun, and her legs wobbled beneath her.

Connor's hands were on her before she could fall. "What are you doing?"

"Bathroom," she muttered, her voice hoarse.

When she tried to move, she wobbled, and he caught her with a gentle grip.

"Let me help you," he said softly.

Harper didn't have the strength to argue. She leaned into him, and he guided her to the bathroom. At the door, she managed a small, painful smile.

"I think I can take it from here."

Connor returned the smile, though it didn't reach his eyes.

"I'll be outside."

After taking care of herself, Harper found him still there, waiting to help her. Connor eased her onto the bed, pulling the covers up to her chin and brushing a stray hair from her forehead.

"I'll be right back," he whispered.

The fever's haze began to envelope her once more. The pull of sleep was strong, but she fought it, desperate for the relief of something cold to drink and the throb of her headache to ease.

When Connor slipped out, a heavy ache settled over her. She didn't want him to be far; a strange, childish fear of being alone came crashing around her. Time stretched endlessly before he returned, holding a bottle of Gatorade and a fresh pack of Advil. He eased her up, his arm a steady anchor, helping Harper drink and swallow the pills.

"Can I get you anything else?" he asked, settling the covers around her.

She shook her head, struggling to hold herself together. Tears burned at the corners of her eyes, hot and unwelcome. Connor's face softened, and his hand rested lightly on her cheek.

"What's wrong?"

Harper blinked, angry at herself. She always cried when she was sick, her emotions raw and unruly.

"I hate this," she choked out. "I hate being sick."

"It's not your fault."

A fresh wave of tears welled up, spilling over before she could stop it. "I might make you late for your dad's funeral," she whispered, voice cracking. "I'll never forgive myself for that."

Connor stayed silent for a moment. She shouldn't have said that, not out loud. After a pause, he kicked off his shoes and lifted the edge of the blanket.

Harper gawked at him. "What are you doing?"

He slipped in beside her, the mattress dipping with his weight.

"You're going to get sick," she murmured, stunned.

Connor let out a scoff. "Please. I'm around sick people all the time. My immune system's basically bulletproof."

She wanted to argue, but her body was too heavy, her head too foggy. She stared at him, unsure what to do with the warmth now radiating from his side of the bed.

"You don't have to do this," she said softly.

"I know," he replied, voice low.

He pulled her close, her cheek resting on the warmth of his chest. His heartbeat was steady, a gentle rhythm beneath her ear. She hesitated before relaxing into him, her fingers curling near his heart.

Connor took her hand, threading his fingers through hers, and smoothed his other hand over her hair.

"I'm not going to miss the funeral," he murmured. "But even if I did, I could never be mad at you."

Harper's mind was a jumbled mess, fever and fear tangling into sharp-edged thoughts. The words slipped out before she could stop them, thick with sleep and fear. "You don't wish you were doing this with Allison?"

Connor's hand stilled in her hair. He eased away just enough to meet her eyes. "Why would you say that? Of course not."

She nestled closer into his chest, her words muffled. "I don't know. My mind's all over the place."

Harper didn't want to think about seeing him with Allison, didn't want to believe the tenderness he showed her now was pity.

Connor pressed his lips to the top of her head, a soft, lingering kiss. "You're crazy."

A ghost of a smile touched her lips. "I know."

The room fell into a comfortable silence, broken only by the hum of the air conditioner and the soft rhythm of Connor's breathing. His presence surrounded her, a steady lifeline cutting through the fever's fog.

Her body, too heavy to fight anymore, gave in at last. Sleep crept in slowly, pulling her down into a restless drift of fever dreams and flickering memories. The only constant was Connor's face appearing again and again, paired with the memory of their last kiss.

Dreaming about Connor eventually jolted Harper from her thoughts. She took in the room, her mind racing when she realized Connor wasn't there. A spike of panic hit her—had he left? She sat up too quickly, the room tilting around her as dizziness threatened to drag her under again.

Thirteen

Day 5: A New Addition

Her eyes swept the room, landing on his suitcase still by the door. Morning sunlight filtered stubbornly through the gap in the curtains, casting a soft glow across the floor. Relief rushed through her. Connor wouldn't have left without it. Before Harper's thoughts could spiral any further, the door creaked open, and Connor stepped inside, carrying two coffee cups and a plastic bag filled with something else.

Their eyes met, and he smiled. "Did I wake you?"

She shook her head. "I woke up a minute ago."

Connor crossed the room toward her and asked, "How do you feel?"

Harper took stock of her body, the lingering ache and heaviness. "I think my fever broke. I still feel kind of off, but I think the worst is over."

"That's good." Connor sat on the edge of the opposite bed,

setting one of the coffees and the bag down on the small side table. "It was a rough night."

Harper's mind immediately went to the worst-case scenario. "What happened?"

He chuckled, the sound low and warm. "You were talking in your sleep."

She gulped. "What did I say?"

Connor paused, his fingers fiddling with the coffee lid. "You said my name a lot."

Harper forced a small smile. "Was I arguing with you?"

"Some of it, yeah." His lips quirked, but he didn't continue.

"And… the other stuff?"

He took a breath, his expression unreadable. "You said you didn't want me to leave. That you wanted only me. And… you told Allison to back off."

Heat rushed to Harper's cheeks. "Wow. I think the fever scrambled my brain."

Connor gave a smirk. "Yeah, probably."

Quiet settled over them, and Harper couldn't tell if he was annoyed or amused. His feelings were so hard to read when it came to her.

She gave a small, nervous laugh. "I hope I didn't, uh, soak you in my sweat."

Connor's head snapped up, his eyes sparkling with laughter. "Only a little." He caught her mortified expression and quickly added, "But it's okay. Really."

She bit her lip and nodded. "I'm going to take a quick shower, and after that, we can leave."

"Oh—before I forget." Connor moved toward her, grabbing the coffee cup from the table. "I stopped by a coffee shop down the street. Figured you could use something comforting after yesterday."

Harper looked at him, surprised. "You didn't have to do that… but thank you."

Their fingers brushed as she took the cup, and for a moment, the air between them felt charged. Harper wondered if he felt it too. If he did, he gave no sign, but shifted his weight and looked away.

"Don't worry about it," he said, voice easy. "Wasn't sure what you preferred, but you struck me as a mocha latte person."

A small, surprised smile tugged at her lips. "I actually love mocha lattes. Somebody dumped one all over my shirt the day we met, remember?"

Recognition flickered across his face, followed by a real, unguarded smile that lit up his entire expression.

"How could I forget that?" he said, shaking his head. "I was so irritated you wanted to stop so early into the trip. But I couldn't help noticing how cute you were when you were pissed."

Harper laughed, the sound was easy and a little surprising. "I *was* pissed. You were laser-focused on getting out of the city while I was sitting there, soaked and miserable."

Connor chuckled at the memory. "Who would've thought this trip would turn out the way it did?"

"Yeah," Harper murmured, her smile lingering as she looked down at her cup. "Who knew?"

"God, that's amazing," she murmured as she took a small sip.

"Good." He gave a small smile before taking a sip of his coffee.

She sat against the pillows, enjoying the warmth of the drink as it worked its way through the last fog of her fever. Her eyes drifted toward the plastic bag beside him.

"What else did you get?"

Connor reached in and pulled out a bottle of water and a

Gatorade. "Figured you were probably dehydrated."

She felt a surge of gratitude. "That was really thoughtful. Thanks."

He shrugged lightly, as if it was no big deal.

They sat in companionable peacefulness, sipping coffee.

After a few more sips, Harper set her cup on the nightstand and stood up to stretch, only to immediately sway slightly.

Connor was on his feet in an instant, catching her by the waist. "Hey—careful. You've been down for a while."

His touch was steady, grounding. But he was too steady, too close. Harper tried not to focus on the way his arm felt around her.

"Thanks. I'll go slower," she said, pulling away gently.

Connor watched her go to her suitcase, digging around for clean clothes before disappearing into the bathroom.

When she stepped back out, skin was flushed from the hot water, limbs loose and light. Her body had finally stopped fighting her. She wore soft shorts and a light t-shirt; she needed something comfortable for the last stretch of the trip.

Connor looked up as she reentered the room. He'd been standing by the window, phone in hand, but slipped it into his pocket the moment he saw her.

"You look better," he said, voice low.

"I feel better," she replied, running a towel through her damp hair. "That shower was a lifesaver."

He nodded, glancing at his phone. "You up for food? Thought we could grab something before we hit the road."

She still felt unsettled. "Maybe something light. Dunkin, if there's one nearby?"

"Yeah. That works."

They moved through the familiar motions: gathering their

things, checking out of the hotel, and stepping out into the cool morning air. Even the short walk to the car left Harper's legs shaky, her body still not fully on board. She was more than relieved when she sank into the passenger seat.

Connor studied her as he slid behind the wheel. "Still with me?"

"Barely," she joked, resting her head against the seat. "But I'll survive."

Connor reached into the backseat and pulled out the same blanket from the day before holding it out to her. "Want this one more time?"

She smiled softly. "Yeah, thanks."

The soft fleece was comforting as she wrapped it around herself. Harper's fingers traced the familiar beaver logo. "Is this from Buc-ee's? When did you get this?"

He gave a sheepish half-smile. "While you were out yesterday. I stopped for gas and snacks. Figured you'd want something soft."

Harper looked over at him with a grateful smile. "That was nice of you. Thank you."

Connor shifted uncomfortably; a grunt of acknowledgment was the only reply.

Harper sank into the passenger seat, the fleece blanket soft on her skin, still carrying the faint scent of clean laundry and gas station coffee. The car rumbled to life beneath them, and as Connor steered them onto the open road, she let herself lean into the steady hum of the engine and the silent, steady presence beside her.

"You know," Harper murmured after a stretch of highway, "you have a better bedside manner than I pictured. I always thought surgeons were supposed to be colder… detached."

Connor's hands flexed slightly. The subtle shift wasn't lost on her.

She immediately regretted saying anything.

"I didn't mean it that way," she said quickly, her voice catching. "I meant… you're different from what I expected."

"It's fine," he said, but the words were clipped, his gaze fixed ahead.

Harper looked out the window, the unease growing within her. "I wasn't trying to make it weird."

Her comments hung in the air.

"I know what you meant," he said at last, in a worn voice.

She exhaled, not sure if she'd repaired the moment or papered over it.

Several miles later, she asked softly, "Do you ever miss it?"

Connor's eyes stayed locked on the road. "Miss what?"

"Surgery. The life you had before."

His jaw tensed. When he didn't answer, Harper added gently, "Do you think you'll ever go back?"

"I don't know if I can." His voice was low, strained.

She hesitated. "Were you good at it?"

He let out a short, humorless laugh. "I was really good. It was the only thing I ever felt certain about."

Connor drifted into an old memory and said. "I remember this old attending used to say if your hands didn't shake before a case, you were dangerous. Mine never did."

Harper let out a quiet chuckle. "Maybe that's the thing worth fighting for."

Connor's shoulders stiffened. "It's not that simple, Harper."

"I know it's not. But maybe it's not impossible either."

He shot her a sharp look. "You think this is about losing a job?"

She blinked, thrown. "I didn't say that."

"It's complicated," he muttered. "It wrecked how I see myself, how everyone saw me. And my dad… I let him down. After the incident. It changed his view of me."

Her voice softened. "Did you ever talk to him about it? About his reaction?"

"Not really. He called. A few months ago. I didn't answer." Connor's mouth pursed. "Now I never can."

She opened her mouth, but nothing came out. Nothing that didn't feel small.

"I keep thinking about how I messed up so much in my professional and personal life," he said, barely above a whisper.

"You can't undo what's in the past," she said carefully. "But you *can* choose what comes next. I know it's cheesy, but it's the truth."

He didn't respond. For a moment, Harper wasn't sure he would.

Finally, he said, "Is that what you're doing? Choosing what's next?"

She turned to him, startled. "What do you mean?"

"I mean this trip. Us. Whatever this is."

Her pulse kicked. "I don't know," she admitted. "I didn't plan for any of this."

"Neither did I," he said. "But it's happening."

The truth of it settled between them.

"Is that why you're still hung up on Allison?" she blurted.

Connor's grip on the wheel tensed. "Don't."

"I saw you two. At the house."

His gaze snapped to hers, stormy. "Saw what, exactly?"

"You let her kiss you."

Emotion rippled across his face—anger, regret, guilt. "Allison kissed me, Harper. I didn't kiss her."

"But you didn't stop her either," Harper said, voice raw.

"I froze," he admitted, his voice breaking around the words. "I wasn't expecting it, and for a second… it felt easier not to make a scene. But that second ended. And I shut it down."

His eyes locked on hers, a rare vulnerability showing. "I never wanted it, Harper. Not once."

A pause stretched before Connor spoke. "Why do you care so much?"

The words carried the weight of a challenge, but his tone revealed a quiet plea.

Harper's voice caught as she whispered, "I don't know."

"Is it because of Nate?" he asked, a thread of something raw in his voice. "Because I'm not him?"

Her head snapped toward him. "No. Don't do that. Don't make this about him."

"What do you want from me, Harper?"

She swallowed, pulse quick and uneven. "I want you to stop hiding from your own life. I want you to see you're still worth something—even after everything."

He didn't answer, eyes locked on the road ahead, jaw clenched and knuckles pale on the wheel.

She spoke once more, her voice low. "You don't have to push everyone away simply because you're scared of what might happen."

He didn't say anything. Only a muscle flexed in his jaw as he stared at the road ahead. Harper didn't expect him to answer. Not now. But she knew he'd heard her.

Neither was willing to prod at the wounds they'd only just laid bare. The hum of the tires blended with the occasional gust of wind brushing the windows.

Up ahead, a giant, sun-faded billboard loomed on the side of the road:

SEE THE WORLD'S LARGEST ARMADILLO – NEXT EXIT

Complete with a cartoonish drawing of a grinning, bucktoothed armadillo wearing a cowboy hat.

Harper let out a sharp, unexpected laugh.

Connor's brow quirked, glancing sideways at her. "What?"

She pointed ahead. "That. It's so stupid."

He smirked despite himself, the corner of his mouth tugging upward. "We should stop."

She stared at him, surprised. "Seriously?"

"Why not?" he shrugged. "You only live once. Might as well see the world's largest taxidermy nightmare."

Harper grinned, a flicker of relief washing over her after hours of strain. "You know, you're full of surprises."

"Don't spread it around," he said dryly, signaling to exit. "I have a reputation to maintain."

They didn't stop, of course. It was only a passing joke, a brief flicker of lightness that didn't require any follow-through. But Harper realized, in that small, ridiculous exchange, how much she'd needed the moment.

The highway stretched ahead in endless ribbons of fading light, the landscape melting into muted tones as the sun dipped lower in the sky. They'd been driving for hours, stopping only briefly for food Harper barely remembered tasting.

Harper eventually went to sleep, and when she stirred awake, the fading taste of fries lingered on her tongue, her limbs stiff.

"How long was I out?" she murmured, voice scratchy.

"A few hours," Connor said, not meeting her eyes. His voice was soft. Careful. "It did you some good."

She didn't say much, only a quiet, steady "Yeah" as the miles slipped by. The signs were starting to shift: new states, new exits, new reminders that this chapter was nearing its final pages.

Harper felt a tingling sense of anxiety wash over her. She had no idea what would happen when this was over. Would they say goodbye at some rental place and never speak again? Or had something started between them?

She didn't have answers. And she doubted Connor did either—if he even wanted them.

An eternity seemed to pass before Connor finally spoke.

"I don't think anyone pushes my buttons the way you do."

Harper looked over at him, taken aback. Her voice came out sharper than she intended. "You say that as if it's a bad thing."

He glanced at her before returning his eyes to the road. "I'm not sure if it's good or bad. It just… is."

Her frustration flared, burning hot inside her. "You need to stop saying things like that."

Connor's jaw flexed. "Like what?"

"You're stuck in some emotional purgatory," she snapped. "One minute you want this—whatever this is—and the next, you shut down. I told you, it's whiplash. I can't keep up."

His fingers gripped the steering wheel a bit harder. "I know. I've been all over the place. That's on me."

But the apology felt too neat. Harper turned toward the window, jaw clenched.

"I'm going to try to sleep a little more," she muttered, not waiting for a response.

"Okay," he said, already knowing the moment between them

had passed.

She curled into the seat, pulling her knees in. Sleep came, but not easily. It was light, restless, slipping through her fingers every time she thought she'd caught hold of it.

Suddenly, a jolt.

The seatbelt pulled tight around Harper, her shoulder slamming lightly into the door. Pain bloomed, sharp and fast, yanking her fully awake.

Connor cursed under his breath.

"What happened?" she asked, fumbling for the buckle.

It was dark now. The trees outside loomed tall and shapeless, shadows swallowing the roadside. The car had stopped at an angle, one side scraped along a slope of dirt and brush.

Connor was out of the car in a flash, his door still swinging open as he strode toward the front.

Harper shoved her door open and stepped into the night. She squinted toward the headlights, their beams diffused by mist.

"What's going on?" she called.

Connor's jaw stiffened, eyes sharp in the darkness. "Something ran out in front of us. I swerved."

Harper moved closer, the gravel crunching underfoot. "You're exhausted. Let me drive for a while."

He barely acknowledged her, mumbling something about insurance. She opened her mouth to reassure him when a soft whimper drifted through the night. Harper's breath caught as she turned toward the sound, her heart quickening.

"Did you hear that?" she asked.

Connor's expression shifted, his frustration giving way to confusion. "What?"

She didn't answer. Instead, she followed the sound to the edge of the road, crouching low. There, huddled and trembling, was a tiny, dust-covered puppy with wide, frightened eyes. The dog, part lab, part golden retriever, stirred a sudden ache deep inside her.

"Connor," Harper called over her shoulder, crouching low in the tall grass beside the road. "Come here. It's a puppy."

When he reached her side and caught sight of the tiny creature, his expression shifted—relief collided with lingering horror.

"Oh my God," he breathed. "I almost hit it."

"But you didn't," she whispered, her voice calm and steady. The puppy sniffed her fingers with curiosity before settling into her lap, as if he'd been waiting just for her. He wagged his tail in frantic, hopeful circles.

Harper smiled, the kind of smile she hadn't worn in days. "Look at him," she said, petting the soft fur behind the puppy's ears. "He's perfect."

Connor crouched beside her, but his tone stayed practical. "He is. But we should call animal control."

Her head snapped up. "What? No. We're not doing that."

He frowned, confused. "Harper, what else are we supposed to do? We can't bring him with us."

"Why not?"

"We're on the road. We're crossing state lines. You don't even know if he belongs to someone."

"He doesn't," she said, holding the puppy close as it snuggled up to her. "There's no collar. No chip tag. Nothing. He was here alone."

Connor dragged his hand over his face, clearly fighting for patience. "And what, you're going to keep him?"

"If I have to."

The look he gave her was somewhere between disbelief and

exasperation. "You're not serious."

"I'm completely serious." She met his gaze, steady and unflinching. "If this is too much for you, I'll call an Uber, find a new rental, and finish the trip myself."

"Harper."

"You said it yourself—you don't know what's going to happen with us. So maybe this is your out."

His expression shifted; a flash of hurt was visible behind the frustration. "That's not fair."

"No," she said, standing now, adjusting the puppy in her arms, "what's not fair is asking me to leave something helpless behind as if it doesn't matter."

Connor exhaled hard through his nose and turned away, pacing a few steps toward the car. "You're being emotional."

The words hit her full force. Harper's pulse spiked. Her voice dropped, rough and raw.

"Better that than numb."

Still cradling the puppy in one arm, she crossed to the driver's side to pop the trunk and yanked her suitcase and bag out with more force than necessary. The sharp sound of tires scraping the pavement echoed too loudly in the night. Connor still hadn't moved.

"Where are you going?" he asked, voice low.

"I told you. I'll figure it out."

The moment Harper reached for her phone, Connor's hand shot out, grabbing it before she could react.

"Connor, give it back!" she snapped, shoving at his shoulder.

"I'm not letting you stay out here by yourself."

"Why not?"

He hesitated, glanced away, and finally said, "Because I care about you, Harper. If I drove off and something happened to you, I wouldn't be able to live with that."

She blinked, caught off guard by the sudden honesty. "Then stop acting as if I'm some detour in your life."

His shoulders slumped as if the weight of everything he'd been holding cracked through. "I don't know how to be the guy who gets it right," he said quietly. "Not when it matters."

She met his eyes, voice softer. "Start small."

The puppy gave a sleepy yawn as it settled on her shoulder, and Connor's gaze dropped to it. He stepped closer and tentatively reached out, letting the pup sniff his fingers before gently scratching its chin. It licked Connor's hand once, tail twitching weakly.

He muttered. "You're really not going to let this go, are you?"

Harper smiled faintly. "Not a chance."

He sighed, a reluctant, amused sound. "You're stubborn."

"Only when it counts."

After a beat, Connor returned Harper's phone and gently reached out to take the puppy from her arms. He held it gingerly. The tiny body sagged into him, and for the first time in hours, something in Connor's posture uncoiled.

"Okay," he said, voice low and warm. "We'll keep the dog."

Relief flooded through her so fast it made her legs weak. She let out a breathless laugh. "Wait—you mean it? No take-backs?"

Connor shot her a look, equal parts fond and exasperated. "Really. But he's your problem."

Harper laughed, bright and disbelieving. "Deal."

Connor met her eyes, and for a brief moment, something unspoken passed between them.

"Let's get your stuff back in the car," he said, cradling the puppy with a carefulness that made her chest ache.

And this time, Harper didn't argue.

As they settled into the car, the puppy nestled on Harper's lap. Connor studied the darkness and said, "We have to stop for the night."

Harper, who had been staring out the window, turned to him. "Are we still good on time?"

Connor tapped through the GPS, nodding. "Yeah. If we leave early tomorrow, we'll make it to California on schedule."

A small smile crossed Harper's lips. "That's a relief."

Connor glanced down at the puppy curled up in Harper's lap. "We should stop at a Target and pick up some things for him before finding a hotel."

Harper raised an eyebrow. "Wow, that's a quick turnaround."

Connor gave a half-smile, a hint of vulnerability slipping through. "I never had a dog growing up."

"Really? No pets at all?"

He shook his head. "Both my parents were allergic to pretty much everything with fur. And when I moved out, I was so busy with school and work that I couldn't even think about getting a pet."

"My parents had this type of dog when I was little," Harper said, a faraway look in her eyes. "His name was Murphy. I adored him. No other dog ever came close to how amazing he was."

Connor reached over, brushing his fingers gently over the puppy's head. Harper felt a warm happiness settle over her.

"What are you going to name him?" Connor asked.

She paused. "I don't know. You got any ideas?"

He mulled it over. "Something tied to this road trip, maybe."

A mischievous smile curled on Harper's lips. "I could call him Wall. You know, as in Not Letting Anyone In."

A genuine chuckle escaped Connor. "Wall. That's good. Not

wrong, either."

She chuckled. "Kidding. How about Lucky?"

Connor looked down at the sleeping puppy. "Yeah. That fits."

Their eyes met, and the moment stretched between them. No teasing. No sharp edges.

Connor pulled into Target as the evening air began to cool. After cracking the windows for Lucky, they crossed the parking lot, and Harper's arm brushed Connor's and he reached for her hand. Neither of them moved away. They slipped inside, grabbed snacks, dog supplies, and the basics to get through the final stretch of the trip.

When they returned to the car, Connor pulled out his phone to search nearby hotels while Harper clipped on Lucky's new collar and harness to take him for a quick walk around the edge of the lot. Ten minutes later, they hit the road again going towards a pet-friendly hotel a few towns over. Harper looked back at Lucky dozing in the rear seat while the scent of plastic Target bags filled the car.

For the first time in a while, Harper didn't feel completely lost.

Fourteen

Day 5: Revelations

It was past nine when they rolled into a stretch of a two-lane road. The town was small, the kind that probably came alive during summer parades and farmers' markets, but now sat tucked into itself, sleepy and golden under streetlamps. Most storefronts were dark, but a restaurant on the corner glowed.

It was a low-slung brick building with wide patio seating, strung with Edison bulbs and the soft murmur of laughter. A chalkboard sign near the entrance read in faded white chalk: *Patio Dog-Friendly. Kitchen Open Late.*

Harper's eyes lit up.

"There," she said, pointing. "That place looks perfect."

"You hungry?"

She shot him a look. "We've had nothing but random snacks and fast food today. I'm still shaking off being sick. I want something that comes on a real plate."

Connor smirked. "I figured you'd hold out for another sad drive-thru burger."

She rolled her eyes, grinning. "Even I have standards."

He gave a laugh, shook his head, and nodded. "Alright. You win."

Harper grinned. "You're the best."

Connor gave a slight shake of his head, but she didn't miss the faint pink that touched his cheeks.

He pulled into a parallel spot a little past the patio entrance. In the back seat, Lucky stirred at the sound of the engine cutting off, his tail thumping lazily.

Harper grabbed his leash and opened the door. As they stepped out, a soft warmth pressed around her. The lights from the patio flickered gently overhead, voices mingling in the background, and music drifted faintly from hidden speakers.

For a brief moment, everything felt real.

As if this were normal, she and Connor were simply another couple stopping for dinner, their dog tired after a hard day. No chaos. No wreckage trailing behind them.

She caught herself smiling and quickly looked away, but not fast enough.

Connor noticed. "What's got you smiling?"

Harper shook her head, trying to play it off. "Nothing."

He stepped closer, close enough that she could smell the clean, woodsy scent of his soap. His eyes found hers—warm brown, steady—and held. For a second, the air around them shifted. Harper wasn't sure if he knew the effect he had on her; how her legs felt wobbly at him being so close. Connor cleared his throat, and she snapped out of it. "Sorry, what did you say?"

"I wanted to know what made you smile," he said, voice lower now. "I like seeing it."

The honesty in his tone made something flutter inside her.

The breeze stirred the scent of grilled onions and fresh-cut grass, and before she could stop herself, the words tumbled out. "I was thinking… it kind of feels as if we're on a real date. With our dog."

She half-winced, unsure how he'd take it—if he'd pull away and retreat behind that guarded look of his. But he didn't. He studied her for a moment, reached up, and brushed a strand of hair behind her ear with quiet, deliberate care.

It should've felt cheesy. Maybe it was. But it also felt… right. Harper's heartbeat hammered beneath her skin, and she wondered if Connor could hear it.

"I like the feeling," he said softly.

Harper's breath caught. She leaned in almost without think-ing.

Lucky's sudden bark shattered the moment, making them both jump.

They pulled away from each other, the moment dissolving into mist.

Connor shifted, glancing toward the restaurant. "I'll grab us a table."

Harper nodded, clutching Lucky's leash. "I'll walk him around for a minute."

She watched Connor walk ahead, his shoulders tense in that way she was beginning to recognize; it was as if he didn't know what to do with softness.

Harper sighed and wandered past the edge of the patio, letting Lucky nose around the patchy grass lining the sidewalk. The lights overhead buzzed softly, casting everything in a honeyed glow.

After Lucky did his business, she headed inside and spotted

Connor at a corner table under a tangle of string lights, the air around him tinted gold. Lucky flopped beneath the table, his nose twitching as a plate of fries passed by.

They ordered drinks, burgers, and fries. By the time the food arrived, the sharp edges of the earlier tension had blended into something easier. The night air cooled, but summer still clung to its edges.

Harper sipped her lemonade, eyes flicking to Connor as he reached for his beer. She didn't want the warmth of their earlier moment to slip too far away.

"You mentioned earlier that your sister's in Europe," she said, casually enough. "What's she doing over there?"

"She works in communications for the government," Connor said, settling into the bench. "She gets assigned overseas for a few weeks at a time."

Harper raised her eyebrows. "That's impressive."

Connor chuckled. "Yeah, she's always had the travel bug. We moved around a lot as kids, so I guess that stuck with her. She enjoys the freedom."

Harper nodded slowly. "Did it stick with you, too?"

Connor considered that. "Not really. I think I got it out of my system early. These days, I'd rather stay in one place. But I do like seeing new things."

Harper smiled into her drink. "Huh. You don't strike me as the spontaneous type."

"I'm not," he said without hesitation. "I prefer knowing what's coming. Having a plan."

"So basically, you're a terrible travel companion," she teased.

He grinned. "And yet, I agreed to share a car with a stranger and to rescue a roadside puppy. I think I've earned at least a little credit."

Harper laughed. "You have a point. I guess you're not the worst."

The table fell silent for a beat, but it wasn't uncomfortable.

Connor scanned her. "You haven't mentioned your family."

Harper's smile faded slightly. "You never asked."

"I'm asking now."

She traced a finger over the condensation on her glass. "There's not much to tell. My parents divorced when I was a teenager. I'm close to my sister. And I love my mom."

Connor said. "Family means a lot to you." She gave a small, knowing smile before he continued. "What about your dad?" he asked gently.

She hesitated, eyes fixed on her fork as she turned it in her hand.

"We're not close," she said at last. "Haven't been for years."

He didn't push, simply waited.

Harper drew in a slow breath. "He's a high-profile lawyer. Loves his job. Loves being impressive. But being a dad?" She shook her head. "I don't think he ever knew what to do with me or my sister."

She looked up and met Connor's eyes, her voice quieter now. "I wasn't who he wanted me to be. I was more into photography, writing... art. And he saw that as a waste. Like I was wasting *his* name."

Connor's expression softened, a flicker of something wounded in his eyes. "Yeah," he murmured, fiddling with the label on his beer. "Some people... don't know how to be what you need."

Harper looked down. For a second, Connor hesitated, unsure if it was okay. His hand found hers anyway, his thumb tracing slow, careful circles over her knuckles.

She swallowed hard before speaking. "It's probably why I stayed with Nate," she said. "He was sharp, polished, and respected. My dad *loved* him. And for a little while, it felt as though I'd finally done something right."

The words hung there, raw and heavier than she meant them to be. Before Connor could say anything, Harper withdrew her hand, suddenly aware of how exposed she'd become.

Connor leaned away, giving her the room without comment. But he didn't let the moment die.

"I get it," he said quietly.

She looked at him.

"I always thought my dad and I were close," he continued. "Until I stopped practicing. Until the accident. That's when I saw it clearly—how much of his love was tied to success. To status. I stopped being useful, and suddenly, I stopped mattering."

Harper didn't speak. She couldn't find the right words.

"It's as if," he added, voice hollow, "you spend your whole life thinking you're safe with someone, and the moment you stumble, they drop you."

Harper exhaled. "Yeah. That sounds about right."

Connor gave a humorless laugh. "Guess we both have the classic 'daddy issues.'"

Harper managed a tired smile. "Maybe that's why we get along so well."

He looked at her, that slight curve returning to his lips. "Could be."

She was about to say more—maybe something sarcastic, maybe something honest—when the waitress appeared with a polite smile, snapping the thread between them.

They both declined dessert, and the waitress nodded, disappearing to grab the check.

Connor sank back into his chair, eyes resting on her. "You've been different today."

Harper raised an eyebrow. "Different how?"

He shrugged, gaze drifting somewhere near her shoulder. "I don't know. Lighter. Like you're not carrying as much."

She blinked, caught off guard. "Maybe… I'm just letting myself enjoy the moment a little more."

He nodded. "That's a good thing."

"Dangerous thing," she murmured, tracing the rim of her glass. "The second I stop guarding myself, I start thinking this"—she gestured vaguely to the table, to him, to everything—"might mean more than it does."

Connor's expression shifted. His shoulders straightened, his posture suddenly alert.

She winced. "Sorry. That came out wrong."

"No," he said quietly. "I get it."

He leaned forward, resting his arms on the table. "I told you… I like having a plan. It keeps me grounded, keeps things from spiraling. But…" He hesitated, his voice quieter now. "I haven't figured out where we fit into that picture yet."

Harper stilled, her fingers sliding down to scratch behind Lucky's ears beneath the table. Anything to keep her gaze from locking onto his. Anything to keep her face from betraying too much.

Connor didn't stop. "I just—" He exhaled. "I need to know where people stand. That's the only way I know how to stay steady. But I do know one thing: I don't want to get to California and say goodbye to you like it's nothing."

Her eyes flicked to his, startled. He went on.

"I know I said this wasn't going to be some movie-style

bonding trip. But… you've made me rethink a lot."

She gave a small, wry smile. "Is it bad that I want more than a quiet goodbye, too?"

His hand found hers. "Not bad at all."

The moment hung suspended between them, fragile and full.

The waitress returned with the check, but before Connor could reach for it, Harper grabbed it. He didn't argue—just gave her that crooked half-smile that said he knew better than to push it.

They left the patio without another word.

The car was silent as they pulled away, the streets quiet and still, lined with closed storefronts and the warm hum of streetlamps.

Lucky curled up in Harper's lap, already snoring. She stroked his fur absently, eyes fixed on the dark glass of the passenger window.

They drove like that for a while, the town fading behind them, headlights stretching out into the dark, chasing nothing but open road.

Harper finally spoke. "You know we kind of hated each other at first, right?"

Connor gave a half-smile. *"Kind of?"*

She looked over at him. "Okay, fine. I *definitely* hated you."

"I remember. The way you looked at me at the airport—as if I'd just ruined everything."

"You weren't exactly friendly, Connor."

He let out a short laugh. "Fair."

A quiet pause. Harper tilted her head, curiosity winning out. "When do you think it changed?"

Connor ran a hand over the scar on his cheek, but not in a tense way, in a thoughtful way. After a moment, he said, "The bar."

She turned to look at him but didn't speak.

"You were laughing," he said. "You looked… free. Lighter than I'd seen you. Your eyes were so alive, and for a second, I forgot everything else."

He didn't finish the sentence, and she didn't ask him to.

"It was a good night," she whispered. "Before everything went sideways."

"Maybe we'll get another one," he said, his gaze lingering on her.

She looked away, pulse tightening. Then he asked, "What about you?"

She hesitated, knowing this moment held more weight than it seemed to. Finally, she looked at him and said, "It was the bar for me, too."

He flicked a glance at her, then returned his eyes to the road.

"I wasn't expecting to feel anything," Harper continued, her voice quieter now as she looked on at the road ahead. "Not after Nate. But that night, I felt safe. And happy. And I didn't even realize how much I'd been missing that."

Connor nodded slowly. "I think part of me didn't want to share a car with you because I had a feeling it'd turn into this."

That made her look over.

He smiled a little, almost self-conscious. "The second you marched up to that rental counter, all annoyed and biting, I looked into those blue eyes and knew I was screwed."

She blinked at him, caught between surprise and something softer.

"I know," he said. "It's cheesy. But it's true."

Harper lifted her hand from Lucky's back and rested it gently on Connor's arm. "I think part of me felt it, too."

He covered her hand with his, giving it a slow, grounding squeeze.

"I don't want to be someone else who hurts you," he said. "I couldn't handle that."

Her voice was low. "You can't think like that."

They let the silence return, but this time it hummed with something unspoken, tender. Her hand stayed beneath his a moment longer, then she slipped it away and returned to petting Lucky.

She turned toward the window, lost in thought. The closer they drew to the hotel, the less sure she was of where they stood.

Check-in was quiet. Barely a word passed between them. The air between them felt stretched thin, like something waiting to break.

The hotel room was small but clean. Two beds, a dresser, and a bathroom with a fan that buzzed faintly in the background. Harper dropped her bag beside the nearest bed, stretching her arms above her head with a tired groan.

"Do you mind watching him while I shower?" she asked, kicking off her shoes.

Connor nodded. "Yeah, I'll take him." Connor picked up Lucky, and they both flopped onto the bed, the TV humming with some sports game.

The hot water was heaven, washing away the lingering remnants of the fever and the road's grit. Harper slipped into fresh clothes and padded into the room, finding Connor and Lucky tangled together on the bed.

A weary smile tugged at her lips. "You two are cute."

Connor's cheeks colored slightly. "He's growing on me."

Harper sat down at the foot of the bed, close enough to run her fingers over Lucky's soft fur.

Connor's hand found her arm, a gentle, grounding touch. "Come here." The contact sent a jolt through her. Part of her wanted to pull away, protect herself. The other part ached to lean in.

She met his eyes, a question lingering between them, and let him guide her closer. Harper moved Lucky a bit and settled into Connor, her back to his chest, with Lucky being a warm, breathing weight in her lap.

The world outside the hotel room seemed to slip away. Connor's fingers drew slow circles on her arm, his breath warm on her neck.

"This is nice," she murmured. And it was, which scared her more than she wanted to admit.

"Yeah," he whispered, his lips brushing the curve of her shoulder.

He pressed a soft kiss to her shoulder, followed by another at the curve of her neck. Harper's hand found his, fingers threading through, grounding herself in something that might not last.

When he turned her to face him, she didn't hesitate.

Their mouths met in a kiss—deeper, hungrier than before. Something had shifted. The charge remained, but Harper couldn't shake the feeling that it was a kiss before a goodbye.

She eased away, resting her forehead gently against his.

"I'm sorry," Connor said, his thumb brushing her cheek. "I keep sending mixed messages."

"You really do." Harper's voice was low, but there was no bitterness in it. "I know things have changed between us, but I'm still left wondering if it's enough."

His eyes searched hers. "You've turned my world upside down, Harper. Part of me wants to say 'screw it,' and promise you everything. But the other part is terrified I'll lose you for good."

Her hand moved to the back of his head, her fingers tangling in his hair. "We'll never know if we don't try."

Connor's jaw tightened. Before he could respond, his phone lit up next to him.

They both startled, the spell breaking.

"I'll ignore it," he said, but Harper's eyes drifted to the screen. Allison.

Harper's stomach dropped, a cold grip constricting deep within her.

"It's your ex," she said, her voice flat. "You should probably take it."

"Harper, it's not—"

She was on her feet in an instant, sliding on her sandals and reaching for Lucky's leash. "I'll take him out. You can take your call."

Her movements were quick and deliberate. The hotel key slid into her pocket, and she was out the door before Connor could say another word.

The cool night air hit her, sharp and sobering. She knew better than to expect more from him now. But with every touch, every moment, she felt herself sinking deeper. And this time, she wasn't sure she'd find her way back out.

Fifteen

Day 5: Attack

Harper wandered around the dimly lit hotel grounds, Lucky trotting beside her, nose to the ground. She was lost in her thoughts, barely noticing the night air nipping at her skin. Her mind was miles away at this point. But a cold, prickling weight settled between her shoulder blades— the unmistakable sense of being watched. She slowed, her pulse leaping as she turned.

A large, greasy-looking man emerged from the shadows a few feet away, moving toward her with slow, deliberate steps. His mouth curled into a cold grin that never touched his eyes.

"What's a pretty thing like you doing out here all alone?" he drawled, his voice thick and oily, laced with something darker.

Harper's pulse slammed in her ears, her fight-or-flight instinct kicking hard. But a steadier voice inside her head whispered: *Keep him talking. Stay calm.*

She took a careful step away, forcing a smile. "Walking my

dog. My boyfriend's waiting for me at the hotel."

The man's grin widened, revealing yellow-stained teeth. "A boyfriend, huh? Then why'd he let you wander off by yourself?"

He stepped closer; she moved again, her fingers tightening around Lucky's leash. Lucky started barking and yanking against her hand. The man's face twisted. "Shut up!" he snapped.

The split-second distraction was all she needed. Harper spun on her heel, ready to run—

But the man's rough hand shot out, grabbing her wrist and yanking her hard. She stumbled, breath caught in her throat. His other hand clamped around the back of her neck, jerking her face inches from his. Her heart slammed against her ribs. Harper couldn't breathe past the sour heat of his breath.

Bile burned up her throat. The stench of sweat, stale beer, and something rotting clung to him, thick and suffocating. She gagged as he leaned in, his grip tightening.

"You made a mistake coming out here alone," he hissed. "Or maybe you wanted this."

Panic crashed over her, but beneath it simmered a spark of rage. She struggled, but he was unyielding, his grip ironclad. She kneed him, hard, but as he doubled over, he dragged her down with him, his weight pinning her to the ground.

Lucky's barking turned savage, teeth flashing as he lunged and sank them into the man's leg. With a grunt, the man jerked his leg and kicked hard, sending Lucky tumbling across the pavement with a sharp yelp.

The sound tore through Harper, but rage flared hotter.

Her left arm was free.

She didn't think—she just swung.

Her fist connected with the man's nose in a clean, solid crack.

His head snapped back, a spray of blood catching the glow of a streetlamp. But he didn't let go.

His hand fumbled into his jacket and reappeared with a knife, the small blade glinting under the dim streetlights. He pressed it to Harper's throat, the sharp edge biting into her skin. Warm blood trickled down her neck.

He whispered vile promises, but her mind shut down, blocking out the words. All she could focus on was surviving. She thrashed beneath him, but every movement made the knife dig deeper. The ground was rough, biting into her as she scraped and clawed.

"Help!" Harper screamed, but his hand smothered her cry. Without hesitation, she bit down hard. His skin broke under her teeth, and he howled, jerking his hand away.

Seizing the moment, she twisted free, scrambling toward the door—but a searing pain ripped through the side of her stomach, just below her ribs. Her momentum faltered, knees buckling. She looked down, stunned to see the man already yanking the blade free from her side, his mouth twisted in a sick, satisfied smile. Warm blood spread beneath her shirt in hot, sticky waves.

The room swayed. Her breath caught.

Still, Harper fought—screaming, kicking, anything to get free. Her nails raked across his cheek, leaving raw, red tracks. He snarled in pain but didn't stop.

Then he drove the knife down again, but this time into her left arm. The impact knocked the wind out of her. Fire bloomed through the muscle, then cold. Her scream cracked in her throat as she crumpled.

The sounds around her became muffled, the world a foggy, detached blur. The night sky spun above her, the taste of copper thick on her tongue. All Harper could hear was the man's labored breathing, Lucky's desperate barking, and the pounding of her own heart.

His hands fumbled at her clothes, but through the haze, she heard her name.

"Harper!"

She thought it was a hallucination, a cruel trick of her fading mind. But the voice grew louder, more real.

Out of nowhere, a shadow slammed into the man, throwing him off her. Harper's head lolled to the side, her body too weak to follow. Connor's fists flew fast and brutal, each strike crushing bone and flesh, until the man crumpled.

Relief washed over her, cold and dizzying.

Connor sank onto his heels, breathing hard, his knuckles stained red. His head snapped toward Harper, and the wildness in his eyes softened.

He crawled to her side, gently lifting her head into his lap. His voice was a rough whisper. "Harper? Are you okay?"

That's when he saw the blood streak along her neck. His breath caught. "Shit. You're bleeding." His eyes scanned her quickly, and he noticed the wound on her neck wasn't deep, but the sight of it still sent a bolt of fear through him.

Harper knew he was asking about more than her physical wounds. She swallowed, fighting the ache rising inside her. "He didn't...he didn't get to..." She forced the words out. "But he stabbed me. My side, my arm... my neck."

Connor's expression shifted. The fear melted away, replaced by the steady, practiced focus of a surgeon. He gently laid her down and pulled off his hoodie, ripped his t-shirt free, and pressed the fabric firmly over her bleeding cuts.

"I've got you," he murmured, his voice steady. His hands

moved with purpose as he dialed 911, setting the phone on speaker.

"Stay with me, Harper."

She blinked slowly, her vision dipping in and out. The dispatcher's voice was a faint buzz as Connor spoke calmly, rattling off their location and her injuries.

Connor continued to hold the shirt tightly over Harper's side, his other hand clamped over the wound on her arm, desperate to stanch the bleeding. "Harper ... I'm so sorry," he whispered, his voice breaking.

She couldn't respond—pain burned in her neck, raw from the man's grip. The sting from her wounds, once dulled by adrenaline, now clawed its way into sharp focus. Harper barely realized that Lucky had curled up next to her. Each second dragged, the agony intensifying, until the wail of sirens cut through the haze.

Red and blue lights flooded the scene. Officers swarmed, cuffing the unconscious man and hauling him into the cruiser. Harper caught snippets of their conversation; something about him being a wanted criminal, but she couldn't bring herself to care. She barely registered the paramedics wrapping her wounds, their hands gentle but businesslike as they loaded her onto the stretcher.

Connor was arguing with them, his voice low and urgent. "I need to go with her. Please. I can't leave her."

"Sir, animals aren't allowed in the ambulance," one of them insisted.

Harper's vision became fuzzy as they prepared to lift her into the ambulance. Panic swelled—the thought of being alone, without Connor, without Lucky, clawed at her. She tried to speak, but only a ragged sound came out.

Connor rushed to her side, Lucky's leash wrapped around his wrist. "I'll put Lucky in the room and meet you at the hospital. I promise." His grip on her hand was firm, his eyes wet with tears. "You won't be alone. I'll be there as soon as I can."

Her fingers wrapped around his, but the moment broke too fast. She watched him shrink into the distance as the ambulance doors closed, his silhouette framed by flashing lights.

The hospital was a whirlwind of white coats, clipped voices, and gloved hands. Cold metal against Harper's ribs. Bright lights burned behind her eyelids. The emergency room doctor spoke in efficient tones about scans and internal damage. Harper nodded because it was easier than talking, easier than facing the sharp throb pulsing through her body or the memory of Connor's face when he found her.

After some poking and prodding, one of the doctors mentioned they were going to put her under anesthesia to close up the knife wounds. Harper simply dipped her head in agreement. Her mind retreated, building walls brick by brick, placing each memory and moment behind glass where she didn't have to feel them yet. The only thing that mattered now was pushing the memory of the disgusting man as far away as possible.

When Harper woke, the world had softened at the edges. The pain was still there, low and dull, but distant enough to breathe. Her eyes fluttered open to find herself in a dim hospital room, the sterile hum of machines filling the air. An IV tugged at her arm. She blinked once, twice—her mind catching up to her body.

The first thing she registered was the warmth of a hand around hers, steady and familiar. Connor. His thumb brushing over her knuckles, over and over.

"Oh, thank God," he exhaled, a breath he must've been holding for hours. "How do you feel?"

Harper swallowed. "Like I was hit by a truck." Her voice was rough. "Really sore." She shifted slightly. "What did the doctors say?"

"That you were lucky." His voice was measured, but thick with emotion. "The knife missed anything serious. Your arm, he hit the bone, but there was no tendon damage. They stitched it. Your side, too. Everything should heal, but you'll be sore for a while. They want you to follow up with a doctor in the next few days."

She gave a slow, reluctant tilt of her head. "Okay." Her eyes wandered up to the ceiling. Relief sank into her bones, cool and heavy. But before she could fully settle into the quiet, Connor's voice pulled her back.

"I'm so sorry, Harper."

Her eyes snapped to his, brows pinching. "What are you talking about?"

He didn't look at her, his gaze fixed on their hands as his fingers curled a little more around hers. "I never should've let you go outside alone. If I hadn't taken that stupid phone call… if I had walked Lucky instead…"

"Connor." She tried to sit up. Pain lanced through her body, and she clenched her teeth. He moved instantly to help, but she waved him off, jaw clenched. "Don't. Don't do that."

"Do what?"

"Make this your fault."

"But it is," he said, voice cracking. "I wasn't there when you needed me."

"You didn't put that knife in his hand," she cut in, sharper than she meant. "You didn't know what was going to happen."

His shoulders sagged, and for a moment, he looked utterly

broken.

She stared at him, her voice faltering. "Don't," Harper whispered, shaking her head. "Don't use this as a reason to shut me out."

Connor didn't answer. He looked at her, and she hated what she saw in his eyes: the shame, the fear, the distance widening between them.

"Seeing you like that…" He swallowed hard. "I thought you were dying. And all I could think about was how I could've stopped it."

She faintly said. "You're hurting me more than that knife ever did." Harper's voice broke on the last word, tears spilling faster than she could stop them. One hand clutched her bandaged side, like she could hold the ache—*all* of it—together.

Connor's hand flinched in hers, but he didn't let go. "What if I hurt you down the line?" he whispered. "What if next time, I screw up so badly there's no coming back from it?"

She turned her head away, tears slipping silently down her cheeks. The sterile scent of antiseptic burned in her nose.

Before he could say anything else, a doctor entered with a clipboard and a brisk smile. Harper gently pulled her hand from Connor's, wiping her face quickly and forcing a nod as the doctor spoke. She heard the words about discharge papers, prescriptions, and follow-up care, but none of them seemed to stick. The doctor's voice faded, swallowed by a rising static in her ears. For a moment, she was there again—that man's face looming too close, breath hot and sour, the press of his grip still phantom-etched into her skin. Her stomach turned. She blinked hard, trying to chase it away.

Connor stayed silent through it all.

The time that followed passed in a haze. A nurse helped

Harper change into a fresh shirt, carefully guiding her stiff limbs as they peeled away the bloodstained remnants of her old one. Thick gauze settled onto her arm and side, anchored with medical tape that tugged at her skin, and a butterfly bandage traced the curve of her neck, neat but jarring. Harper winced with every movement, the ache deep and pulsing beneath the sterile white layers. She drifted through the room as Connor filled out paperwork a few feet away, hovering but never truly meeting her eyes.

By the time they stepped out into the cool night air, it was well past 3 a.m. The parking lot was primarily empty and silent under flickering streetlights.

Connor opened the car door for her. Harper climbed in slowly, every movement stiff and aching. She saw him reaching closer to hold her steady.

"I can do it," she said flatly.

He didn't argue. But Harper noticed the look on his face and the way it crumpled ever so slightly.

The drive to the hotel was silent, tension thick in the air. At the door, Lucky bounded over. Harper knelt carefully, burying her face in his fur. The warmth of him was a balm in the lingering pain.

Connor set down a bottle of pills on the counter. "You named him right."

She looked up. "Why's that?"

"I almost took a different path while looking for you. But I heard Lucky barking. He led me to you."

A sharp pang gripped her. "Everything happens for a reason."

He stayed quiet, busying himself with unpacking their things. Harper watched him, the distance between them widening.

"So, we're still leaving early in the morning?" she asked.

Connor stopped for a beat. "We can go later. You should rest."

"No." Her voice was firm. "I want to get to California." Away from him. Away from the ache of wanting something he wouldn't give.

"Harper..." He took a step forward, but she raised a hand, halting him.

"I don't want to hear it, Connor. You've made things pretty clear. I want to move on and start my life."

They stood looking at each other, the air thick with things neither of them could find the words for.

Harper was too tired for this and slipped under the bed covers, wanting to hide from everything. "Goodnight, Harper," Connor said from across the room.

She didn't answer. Connor stood there in silence, the light clicking off after a lingering pause, leaving them both adrift in darkness.

Sixteen

Day 6: Aftermath

The alarm's shrill blare yanked Harper awake. She lay still, disoriented, until the dull ache in her side reminded her where she was. The clock read 6:30 a.m., too early, too soon. Her body protested as she shifted to sit up, muscles stiff and aching, the gauze wrapped around her arm pulling uncomfortably with the movement. The butterfly bandage on her neck and the larger one on her side tugged at her skin. She winced, trying not to disturb the IV bruises on her arm as she swung her legs over the side of the bed.

Harper watched as Connor stirred in the other bed, his movements slow and reluctant as he began to wake. She grabbed some clothes from her suitcase and slipped into the bathroom, the dim light casting shadows under her tired eyes. The mirror reflected her face: pale, drawn, and slightly swollen from the night's events. She quickly splashed water on her face before gathering her things.

She wore a loose t-shirt that didn't hide the bandages and bruises along her neck. When she walked out she saw that Connor was in his typical uniform of a plain tee and jeans.

Neither Connor nor Harper was in the mood for words after the heaviness of the night before. Harper winced with each step as she walked to the door; the tight bandages were a reminder of everything that had happened. They took Lucky for a quick walk, the puppy's little paws clicking on the pavement, fleeting normalcy in the middle of the tension. She turned towards Connor, his face unreadable in the dim morning light. She wanted to ask what he was thinking and if he regretted the words they'd left unfinished in the dark. But she didn't.

Inside the car, silence clung to them as they drove to a bagel place, grabbed a quick bite, and merged onto the highway again. Hours of asphalt unraveled ahead, long and empty, California still a distant promise.

The plan was simple: Connor would drop Harper off at her friend's place and then he would head to his father's funeral.

Connor exhaled slowly. Harper stole a glance his way, waiting, hoping. But his eyes stayed fixed on the road, jaw tight.

The quiet deepened. Harper leaned into it, letting the soft drone of tires on pavement swallow whatever she'd wanted to say.

As they approached the final leg of their journey, Harper checked the GPS. The estimated arrival time crept ever upward. "There's a slowdown," she murmured.

Connor's jaw flexed, and she could feel the edge of his frustration in the way his knuckles gripped the steering wheel. The GPS insisted they were still on the fastest route, but soon, the line of brake lights ahead said everything. Bumper-to-bumper traffic, a sudden halt to any sense of forward motion. Time dragged, each minute heavier than the one before, and Harper could see the pressure pressing down on Connor.

She swallowed hard and cleared her throat. "Let's go straight to the funeral," she said softly. "You can drop me off afterward."

Connor's eyes flickered to her, his expression conflicted, but no words came for a moment. "Are you sure?" he asked, his voice low and hesitant, "I texted my sister earlier and told her I'd probably be late."

"Yes," she murmured. "You can't miss all of it. If you don't want me there, I'll stay in the car."

His features eased, just briefly, before he shook his head. "Are you crazy?" he said, his voice quieter now, edged with concern. "You're not staying in the car." Connor looked at her, something softer in his eyes. "It'll be nice to have you there."

Harper held his eyes, holding it a beat too long. A fragile understanding flickered between them. She couldn't quite bring herself to reach for him, but her voice was steady. "I'm here. For whatever you need."

Connor's eyes met hers again. "You have no idea what that means to me."

She sighed. Words like that felt dangerous. They dangled hope in front of her, only to snatch it away. She couldn't trust it, especially not if he planned to walk away when this was all over.

They didn't speak until Connor put the funeral home's address into the GPS. The traffic eased, and soon, they rolled into the sun-soaked streets of a quintessential California town. Palm trees swayed beneath a perfect blue sky, and Harper found herself squinting at the beaming facades of gorgeous houses.

"Is it nice being back here?" she asked.

Connor nodded. "I miss it."

Words dried up as their destination loomed closer. Harper's pulse quickened, nerves prickling under her skin. She scanned their clothes, realizing how out of place they'd be. Everyone else would look crisp, polished, and appropriately somber.

"We aren't dressed for a funeral," she murmured, tugging at her wrinkled shirt.

Connor's lips quirked into a half-smile. "It's okay. My family will be happy I'm there."

She pulled Lucky closer, burying her fingers into his fur for a small comfort.

When they arrived at the church, it was clear that Connor's father had been well-loved. Although Harper couldn't feel a small twinge of anger at how he had given up on Connor when he was at his lowest. The crowd was thick, people gathered in clusters, and Harper's anxiety spiked as she realized they had arrived in time for the burial. The moment's weight pressed in on her.

Connor opened her door, his expression distant, yet his touch was gentle as he helped her out of the car. "Thanks," she murmured. He gave a nod, his eyes scanning the crowd, his mind elsewhere.

She took Lucky to a patch of grass, giving the puppy a moment to settle before they joined the funeral procession. Connor moved ahead of Harper, but his hand found hers and remained firmly there, an anchor in the tide of uncertainty.

They walked toward the gathering of mourners, and Harper's eyes landed on a petite woman with soft brown eyes and a welcoming smile: Connor's mother. The resemblance between them was undeniable, in the gentle curve of her mouth and the way her eyes lit up when she saw Connor.

Next to Connor's mom stood a blonde woman, whom Harper assumed was his sister. His mother's arms wrapped around him instantly, her face crumpling in a way that made Harper's chest ache. His sister's arms squeezed him quickly, and Harper saw the sparkle of tears threatening to fall. Connor gestured for Harper to join them. As she moved closer, she offered a tentative smile, her presence uneasy in this deeply personal moment.

"This is who I've been sharing the car with," Connor said, his voice warm despite the somber surroundings. "Harper, meet my mom, Betty, and my sister, Stacy."

Harper shook their hands, their grips soft but firm. "It's nice to meet you both. I'm so sorry for your loss."

Betty and Stacy murmured their thanks. Betty's voice was gentle, almost soothing. "Thanks for helping get Connor here," she said, her eyes soft with gratitude.

Harper managed a small smile. "It's been an adventure," she replied.

Stacy chuckled lightly. "When it comes to my brother, I believe that," she said, offering a knowing look that helped Harper ease up a bit.

As the introductions continued, faces and names blurred together, each one layering more weight onto the moment. When the group began to move toward the cemetery, Connor lingered with his family while the priest stepped forward to begin the burial prayers. Harper, unsure of where to stand, hovered at the edge of the crowd.

Connor noticed and reached for her, gently threading his fingers through her right hand. "I want you with me," he said quietly.

Harper squeezed his hand, the simple contact grounding her.

They stood side by side, Lucky sitting calmly at her feet as if the small dog understood the gravity of the moment. The ocean breeze tousled her hair, but it did little to ease the weight in the air.

When the prayers ended, family members stepped forward one by one to touch the casket. Harper expected Connor to let go, but he didn't. Instead, he held on tighter and guided her with him.

With her right hand in his, she lifted her left—awkwardly, carefully. Pain flared in her arm, the dull throb of the healing wound sharp now with movement. But she didn't let go of Connor. She wouldn't.

Her fingertips brushed the cool surface of the casket. When she looked up at Connor beside her, her breath caught. A single tear clung to his lashes, a fracture in his composed exterior that said everything he couldn't.

And in that quiet, exposed moment, Harper knew—without question—that she'd walk through fire before she'd let go of his hand.

The ceremony concluded, and family and friends were told to head to Connor's parents' beach house for dinner.

The weight of the funeral clung to them as they walked back to the car, each step slow, reluctant. Neither spoke as Connor pulled onto the road, the winding streets of the beach town blurring past the windows. The hum of the tires and the distant crash of waves filled the quiet between them.

Harper stole a glance at Connor, his profile carved in the golden slant of late afternoon light. His jaw was tight, his brows drawn, and she could see in the faraway look in his eyes that he was somewhere else entirely.

"How are you holding up?" she asked gently.

Connor didn't answer right away. His eyes stayed on the road, but his fingers flexed against the leather. "I'm not sure," he said. "It doesn't feel real yet. I kept thinking he'd be standing there when we pulled up. Arms crossed, probably judging me for being late."

Harper gave a soft, sympathetic smile. "He sounded like a presence."

"He was," Connor murmured. "Impossible to please." He paused, letting out a slow breath. "But he was still my dad."

Harper shifted in her seat, wincing as the movement tugged at her left side. Still, she reached across her body with her right hand and let her fingers brush Connor's arm. "You don't have to figure it all out today."

He glanced over, then turned his palm up and threaded his fingers through hers. The tight line in his shoulders loosened just slightly. "I didn't think having you here would matter this much," he said, voice low. "But it does."

She gave his hand a gentle squeeze, though a sharp throb shot through her side. She didn't let go.

As the car crested the final bend, the house came into view. Harper's breath caught.

Perched above the bluff, the beach house stood tall and striking. The pale stone walls were washed in warm light, floor-to-ceiling windows catching glints of the sea, and wild greenery dancing in the coastal breeze. It looked less like a family home and more like something lifted from a magazine spread.

Connor pulled into the drive and shut off the engine, but neither of them moved right away.

"You never said your parents lived in a place like this," Harper murmured, her eyes still fixed on the view.

Connor gave her a small, almost sheepish smile. "I don't brag.

My parents' money is theirs, and I've had people assume I'm rolling in it once they see this place."

"Aren't you, though?" Harper asked, only half-joking.

Connor shifted in his seat, his discomfort evident. "I do okay."

"So you're the secretly rich, emotionally unavailable type. I should've guessed." She studied his profile as they walked toward the front of the house. "So, what exactly did your parents do?"

"They were behind the scenes in the movie industry. Smart with their investments."

She looked thoughtful. "And you? I'm guessing you've been smart with your investments, too."

He only responded with a curt nod, his expression unreadable.

Inside, the house was almost too perfect. The sunlight spilled across polished floors, and every corner seemed touched by thoughtful design. Coastal blues and warm woods gave the space a magazine-worthy elegance, but Harper couldn't shake the feeling that she didn't quite belong. The ceilings felt too high, the rooms too quiet, like she might knock something over just by breathing.

Connor spotted his mother near the kitchen, and her expression softened the moment she saw them.

"Thank you again for being here," she said warmly, reaching out to squeeze Harper's hand.

Harper returned a small, sincere smile. "Of course. Your home is beautiful."

Connor's mom gave a quiet, knowing nod, her eyes lingering for a moment before she turned to rejoin the others.

Connor leaned in slightly. "I'm going to say hi to a few relatives."

Harper nodded, her throat tight. "Yeah. I'll just—" She gestured vaguely toward the back of the house. "I need a minute."

She didn't wait for him to answer. The walls felt too close, the air too still. Slipping out the glass doors, Harper stepped into the salt-kissed breeze before the house could swallow her whole.

She found the sliding doors and stepped out with Lucky at her heels. The moment the ocean breeze touched her skin, she let out a breath she hadn't realized she was holding. Harper slipped off her shoes and walked across the smooth flagstone, down toward the edge of the sand.

The beach yawned wide and empty, the tide whispering its way in. Cool grains of sand clung to her feet as she wandered along the waterline, letting Lucky nose through bits of seaweed and shell.

She was watching the waves roll in when she felt someone approaching from behind. Turning, she saw a woman coming, Connor's sister, Stacy.

"Hey," Stacy greeted softly, offering a smile. "Mind if I join you?"

Harper shook her head. "Not at all."

They stood side by side for a moment, watching Lucky sniff at bits of seaweed tangled in the tide.

"Did this happen on the trip?" Stacy asked, her eyes flicking to the bandages peeking out from beneath Harper's sleeve and her neck.

Harper paused before giving a nod. "Yeah. A rough stop on the way."

Stacy's brow furrowed slightly, but she didn't press. Harper quickly shifted the focus.

"It's healing, though. How are you holding up?"

Stacy exhaled, her face fixed on the horizon. "I'm… managing. My dad was complicated, but he was still Dad, you know?"

Harper nodded. "Connor mentioned that. He said your dad was tough."

A hum of acknowledgment passed between them.

Stacy glanced over. "He seems really comfortable with you."

Harper looked down at the sand. "He's been… good company." She hesitated. "Easier to be around than most people."

"That's not something I've heard said about him in ages," Stacy said with a soft laugh. "The past few years have been hard. After everything that happened with Connor—and the fallout with my dad—I don't think he realized how much he's been carrying."

Harper's heart clenched. "He mentioned what happened. I can tell it still bothers him a lot."

Stacy's expression changed. "He feels things deeply. Always has. Even when he tries not to show it." She looked away, her voice gentler now. "I hope whoever ends up in his life knows how to handle him. Not because he's fragile—he isn't—but because when Connor loves, he's all in. And when it breaks… it takes him a while to recover."

Harper's lips parted, but no words came out. She offered a tight smile instead.

Stacy noticed the change and softened her tone. "Sorry, I didn't mean to make that sound as if it were a warning. He's my brother—I care about him."

"No, it's okay," Harper said quietly. "You're looking out for him."

Stacy smiled, more relaxed now. "Exactly." She gave Lucky a scratch behind the ears. "Well… I'll let you get back to your walk. It was good talking to you."

"Same," Harper said.

Stacy turned and headed toward the house. Harper stood still, the breeze tugging at her hair, her thoughts suddenly louder than the crashing surf.

Stacy hadn't accused her of anything. She hadn't needed to.

The weight of everything, Connor's grief, his trust, the tenderness growing between them, pressed in all at once. Stacy's words echoed in her head, and they weren't exactly a warning, but a reminder of the kind of man Connor was. Loyal. Deep-feeling. Quietly vulnerable. And it left Harper with a growing sense of responsibility she wasn't sure she was ready to carry.

She pulled out her phone and stared at the screen, her thumb hesitating. After a brief pause, she tapped her friend's name and lifted the phone to her ear.

"Hey, Sydney. Can you come pick me up?" Harper's voice barely rose above the sound of the surf, the words splintering on her tongue. "I… I think I need to get out of here."

Sydney's voice was warm and concerned, asking no questions, only promising to be there soon. Harper hung up, texted Sydney the address, and stared out at the sea, the horizon hazy as the pressure of her decision bore down on her.

She settled onto the cool sand beside Lucky, who pressed softly into her side. Harper ran a hand through his fur, grounding herself in the comfort of his presence. "We had a good run, didn't we?" she whispered. Her voice cracked. She let out a shaky laugh that barely made it past her lips.

The sun dipped lower, painting the waves with a fiery glow. Eventually, the breeze chilled her skin, and she gave a gentle tug on Lucky's leash. "Come on, buddy."

They walked toward the house in silence. Harper hesitated

at the back door, her hand hovering before she finally pushed it open and stepped inside. Laughter floated from the kitchen. She could hear Connor's voice among the others, and something fragile cracked inside her.

She followed the sound and found him talking with his mother. Betty caught sight of her first; her eyes softened, and she nudged Connor gently.

He turned and smiled, warm and easy. "Hey. You okay?"

Harper forced a small, tired smile. "I need to grab my stuff," she said quietly. "My friend's on her way."

Connor blinked, caught off guard. "Wait… you're leaving now?"

She nodded, voice steady but distant. "Yeah."

Harper glanced at Betty again. "I'm sorry, again, for your loss." Betty's glance shifted between Harper and Connor, puzzled.

Turning back to Connor, Harper's voice dropped. "Can you walk me out?"

He hesitated, like he was frozen in place, then nodded slowly. They moved toward the front of the house, the light fading outside.

Once on the porch, Connor's hands reached out, resting lightly on her shoulders, turning her toward him which was the last thing she wanted.

"I don't get it," he said, disbelief threading through his voice. "Why now? That wasn't the plan."

Harper shook her head. "I have to go."

His fingers tightened. "I thought we'd have time to talk in the car. We still do."

She looked away, swallowing hard. "Connor… we were supposed to be strangers sharing a ride. That's it. But things got messy and complicated."

"So we figure it out," he said, voice low but firm.

"I'm not ready," she whispered. "And I don't think you are either."

Connor's brow furrowed. "That's not how it felt. I thought things changed."

"I know," she admitted. "But what if that's just the rush of these last two days? What happens when you have space to think? This… this is too much. We fight too much. We're too different."

He stared at her, searching. "That's it? Because we argue, you're walking away?"

Harper's resolve wavered. "I'm leaving because I care, Connor. If I stay, I'll fall harder, and one of us will break. I don't think either of us can carry that right now."

His voice cracked as he stepped closer. "You think I don't care already?"

"I don't know exactly how you feel," she whispered. "And I can't keep guessing."

At that moment, a car rolled up. Sydney's face appeared through the window, curious but patient. Lucky sat calmly beside Harper, his tail thumping softly against the porch floor.

"Can you help me grab my things?" Harper asked, voice low.

Connor walked toward the car and opened the trunk to grab Harper's suitcase, his motions tight, deliberate. Harper reached for her backpack, fingers brushing the soft blanket he'd given her when she was sick. She pulled it close, holding it like a lifeline.

He lifted Harper's suitcase and placed it carefully in the back of Sydney's car, then looked at her with searching eyes. "So… this is it?"

Her hand paused on the door handle. Staying would be easy—

too easy—but she shook her head. When she met his gaze, something inside her broke quietly.

"Text me when you turn the car in. I'll send my half. After that… you won't hear from me."

Harper started to turn, but Connor's hand caught hers before she could go.

"I don't want it to end like this," he said, voice rough, raw.

"Neither do I," she whispered. "But it has to."

Her voice faltered as she added, "You were good for me, Connor."

"Thank you," she whispered, pressing a soft kiss to his cheek before the weight of the moment swallowed them both.

She turned away quickly, not wanting him to see the tears threatening to fall.

Sydney nodded gently from the driver's seat as Harper climbed in, Lucky settling at her feet. She stared straight ahead as the car pulled away.

The beach house faded behind her, blurred by the tears she no longer tried to hold back.

Harper didn't look back. But her fingers clutched the blanket tightly; a last tether to a trip that had changed everything.

Seventeen

Epilogue

ime was supposed to heal all wounds. That's what
Harper kept telling herself as she sat in the corner
booth of the coffee shop, her eyes drifting to the
window without really seeing. She didn't realize she was staring
until she caught sight of a couple at the crosswalk—a tall, dark-
haired guy and a blonde beside him.

Harper shook her head, dragging herself back to the present.
She needed to stop doing this.

Every tall, brown-haired stranger she passed over the last
three months earned a second look. And every time, some
foolish, stubborn part of her hoped it would be Connor.

It never was.

With a sigh, she turned to her laptop. The lifestyle brand that
had brought her out to California loved her work so much that
they'd offered her a full-time job within two weeks. Hybrid
hours. Good pay. She split her days among her friend Sydney's

apartment, this coffee shop, and the nearby office. It was a steady, safe thing.

She should've been happy.

And she was. Mostly.

Moving out of Sydney's place was next on the list, but signing a lease felt heavier than it should—as if it meant closing a door she wasn't ready to lock. Harper told herself it was about New York and that she'd miss the buzz of the city where anything felt possible.

But deep down, she knew it wasn't about the city.

Connor's family was an hour up the coast, but this wasn't his home anymore. New York was, and deep down inside, Harper knew part of her was hoping that if she returned to New York, she'd somehow run into him.

It was ridiculous to think about. She knew that.

After leaving his parents' house, the only thing between them had been a single, impersonal text about splitting the car expenses. Connor had confirmed the Venmo. That was it. No calls. No late-night texts. No breadcrumbs to follow. Harper did the occasional, shameful peek at his Venmo feed—and she hated herself every time she did it.

He wasn't going to reach out.

He didn't want to.

So why was she still hoping?

The question pierced her thoughts, refusing to let go. Frustration surged, and Harper snapped her laptop shut. *Enough.* It was time to let go.

From now on, no more Connor. No more thinking about that trip. No more replaying those nights in nowhere towns or those perfect, stolen moments they had.

Harper was done.

And to her surprise, the thought didn't shatter her. She felt calm.

She gathered her things and stepped out of the coffee shop, the cool coastal breeze touching her skin. It felt good. Clean. A reset she hadn't realized she needed.

She was so done watching for tall strangers that she didn't even notice a man stepping out of a nearby car, his gaze catching on her, a flicker of hesitation crossing his face before he froze in place.

Harper kept walking.

When she pushed open Sydney's apartment door, Lucky came bounding toward her as if she'd been gone a year, tongue out, tail wagging. Harper kicked off her shoes, dropped her keys and bag by the door, and crouched to scratch under his chin—his favorite spot. His easy, unconditional joy was impossible not to absorb.

He was also a living reminder of where and when she'd found him. But Harper wasn't going to think about that now.

In the kitchen, Sydney was pulling a snack from the fridge, wearing her comfy clothes and listening to a podcast on her phone.

She glanced up, a flicker of something passed over her face before she slipped her phone out of sight. "So… how was the coffee shop?"

Harper gave her a half-smile. "Good. Finished early."

Sydney gave her a quick, thoughtful look. "Nice. I'm off soon. Wanna grab some dinner? It's Friday."

Harper crossed to the cabinet and grabbed a treat for Lucky. As she handed it to him, the words came out before she could overthink them.

"Actually… I was thinking we could head to your brother's

bar tonight. It's the soft opening, right?"

Sydney froze mid-sip, eyes wide. "Wait—you actually want to go out and drink?"

Harper smiled, feeling an unfamiliar spark ignite within her. "Yeah. I'm ready. I need to get out."

Sydney's face broke into a smile as she approached and enveloped Harper in a close hug. "God, I'm so happy to hear you say that. We're gonna have the best night."

Harper grinned. "I'm excited."

Sydney stepped back. "What do you say we go get blowouts and get fabulous?"

Harper laughed a genuine, unforced laugh before nodding. "Let's do it."

The afternoon went by in the way good days do. It was the kind of easy joy Harper hadn't felt in a long time.

They got their blowouts, grabbed a quick dinner, and got ready together—doing their makeup side by side, just like they used to.

Harper pulled on a light blue sweater that slipped off one shoulder, accentuating her eyes. Paired with jeans and loose waves, it felt natural. Effortless.

When Sydney appeared in a dress and a light jacket, she was typing something out on her phone. She glanced up, something unreadable in her eyes, before tucking the phone away.

"You ready?"

Harper took a breath. "Ready."

They gave Lucky one last scratch and headed out. The streets glowed with hazy, golden light, the air thick with the scent of saltwater. Music drifted from open windows as they pulled up to the bar.

The neon sign hummed, waves crashing softly in the distance.

And for the first time in months, Harper wasn't thinking about Connor.

At least… not yet.

Inside, the place was alive. Music thumped, glasses clinked, and laughter rolled through conversations. They went up to the bar, and Sydney's brother had drinks in their hands within minutes. They danced, and they laughed.

It wasn't perfect. But it was something.

And for a little while, it was enough.

Until it wasn't.

The high started to fade. The music slowed, and the couples leaning in close made the room feel too small.

A familiar ache pressed in on Harper.

She forced a smile and leaned into Sydney. "Hey, I'm gonna take a walk on the beach."

Sydney barely glanced over, her eyes locked in with a guy across the bar. 'You good?'

"I'm good," Harper lied.

She slipped outside.

The night air hit her skin, stealing her breath for a second. String lights swayed above the patio, memories pressing. She crossed the patio fast, shoes in hand, heading for the water.

The beach was quiet, the steady crash of waves the only sound. The full moon hung high, casting silver light over the sand. Harper wrapped her arms around herself, staring out at the endless dark water.

The tears hit before she could stop them.

She didn't know how long she stood there before her legs gave out and the flood of the past crashed over her.

When the tears slowed, she scrubbed at her face and pushed to her feet, brushing sand from her jeans. She turned back toward the bar, and that's when she saw him.

A tall figure moved down the beach, heading straight for her.

For one unhinged second, she thought she was imagining it. But as he came closer, there was no mistake.

Connor.

Her heart lurched.

He slowed as he caught sight of her face, his expression stiffening.

"Harper?" His voice was rough, hesitant.

She swallowed hard. "Connor?"

He nodded, and she felt so many questions flooding her mind.

"What... how... how are you here?"

He rubbed the back of his neck. "I saw your friend's name on Venmo. Looked her up. Took me a while to work up the nerve to message her."

Harper paused for a second. *Sydney.* Her weird vibe earlier. The look she had on her face before they left. "Today?"

Connor looked at her and said. "I was supposed to talk to you at the coffee shop."

Her stomach flipped. "Why didn't you?"

He exhaled. "You looked happy. I didn't want to ruin it."

The waves filled the space between them.

"How've you been?" he asked, stepping closer.

"I've been... okay," she managed, "And you?"

Connor gave a humorless smile. "I've been awful."

It knocked the breath from her lungs.

"Why? Is it your family, or–"

"No." He shook his head. "They're fine. Things haven't been the same. Not since you."

Harper bit her lip, blinking fast. "Connor." She shook her head and said, "I can't do this."

He held up his hand to stop her from saying anything else, and he said, "I need to get some things off my chest." Harper looked at him and nodded. He went on, "I tried to convince myself it was only a road trip. That it didn't mean anything." His voice cracked. "But it did. It meant everything."

A raw ache coiled deep inside her.

"I see you everywhere," Connor said. "Every time I get in my car, I half expect you to be there. Every blonde I pass, I hope it's you. Every day I want to call you."

A tear slid down her cheek. He hesitated, but walked closer to her and brushed the tear away with his thumb.

"I know it's crazy," he whispered. "I know you've probably moved on. But I haven't. I can't."

Harper closed her eyes, her hand covering his. "I haven't stopped thinking about you either. That trip... it changed everything for me, too."

His breath hitched, breaking into a crooked grin. "Thank God."

Connor moved closer, but Harper pulled away just enough to hold her ground. His brow furrowed.

"I can't do this if you're going to change your mind," she said. "If you're going to get in your head and decide we can't be something. I can't go through that again."

He held her eyes, steady and certain. "Harper... these last few months without you have been hell. I've never felt emptier. You made me feel alive. You saw me. You believed in me when I didn't believe in myself. And I swear to God, I'm not walking away from that twice."

She exhaled, the tension inside her loosening in one aching, hopeful beat.

The tears came fast now, sharp and unstoppable.

"I don't ever want to say goodbye to you," Harper whispered, her voice breaking around the words.

Something in Connor's expression shattered. In the next breath, he closed the space between them, his hand finding the back of her head, and kissed her with the desperation of a man drowning—desperate, messy, real. All the months of missing her, loving her in silence, poured out in that impossible, perfect kiss.

Harper melted into him, her arms looping around his neck, his hands tangling in her hair with a grip that promised he wouldn't let go. It was as if no time had passed at all.

When they came up for air, their foreheads touched, breath mingling, both of them wrecked in the best way.

Connor gave a crooked, breathless grin. "Well… that went better than I expected."

Harper let out a wet, shaky laugh. "If I wake up and this is some tequila dream, I swear to God…"

He kissed her slower this time, lingering as though he couldn't quite believe it either. "It's real. I'm here. I'm not going anywhere."

"Promise?" she asked, her voice small but steady.

Another kiss. "Promise."

She smiled through the last of her tears, groaning softly. "I'm going to kill Sydney for not warning me."

Connor chuckled, brushing his thumb over her cheek. "Don't be mad. I made her swear. I wasn't leaving without seeing you first."

Harper grinned, tracing her fingertips along the line of his jaw, committing him to memory as if she hadn't already memorized him months ago. "So… what now?"

Connor cupped her face, his eyes warm and steady in a way

that left no room for doubt. "Whatever you want, Harper."

And for the first time in months, she didn't hesitate.

"I want you, Connor."

His smile was slow, sure—exactly what she'd been missing.

"Then that's what you'll have."

And when he kissed her again, everything inside Harper finally, finally felt right.

THE END

About the Author

Laura Tapper writes emotional, messy fiction about complicated people trying to figure life out one mistake at a time. When she's not working on her next book, you can find her hanging out with her family, going on walks, and staying up way too late reading.

Follow her on Instagram: **@lauratypedthis**

Or contact her: **lauratypedthis@gmail.com**

Leave a Review

If you enjoyed *What Happens In The End?*, I'd be so grateful if you left a quick review on **Amazon** and **Goodreads**. Reader reviews help indie authors more than you know, and I'd love to hear what you thought!

You can connect with me on:

🌐 https://lauratapper.carrd.co

Subscribe to my newsletter:

✉ https://lauratypedthis.substack.com